# THE WITCH AND THE ALIEN

## JULIET GARDIN

This is a work of fiction. Names, characters, places, and incidents are products of the author's imagination or are used fictitiously and are not to be construed as real. Any resemblance to actual events, locations, organizations, or persons, living or dead, is entirely coincidental.

**World Castle Publishing, LLC**
Pensacola, Florida
Copyright © Juliet Cardin 2022
Hardback ISBN: 9798369744277
Paperback ISBN: 9781960076106
eBook ISBN: 9781960076113
First Edition World Castle Publishing, LLC, December 19, 2023
http://www.worldcastlepublishing.com
**Licensing Notes**
Cover: Karen Fuller

Editor: Karen Fuller

# PROLOGUE

"Jazel! Are you here?" My voice sounded overly loud, disturbing the silence of the small, dark house. The back room was my destination. If she was anywhere, it would be there.

Sure enough, I found her bent over the antique table that took up more than half the room. Strong scents greeted my nostrils. Drying plants dangled from the ceiling and overflowed from shelves, seeming to reach out to welcome me with spidery hands.

Jazel's ancient, knowing eyes flicked up, taking in my haggard appearance in one glance. My dirty hands and knees revealing I'd been up to no good

"What have you done now?" she asked, releasing a sigh. Her long, crinkly nest of gray hair was tied back, keeping it out of her way.

Lying would be useless. She'd see through me in an instant. I shrugged my shoulders and stared at the hole in my sneakers instead.

She shook her head and turned her attention back to the table. Spread out was a bunch of smelly plants and herbs, a few straight twigs, and a clump of earth. My own problems suddenly jumped from my mind.

"What you got cooking up?" I asked. Her old tome of spells lay open, and I came closer to steal a peek.

"Never you mind, Petal. This doesn't concern you."

Laid across the open pages of the book, so fine you could hardly see them, were three mid-length grayish hairs. "Whose are those?"

She glared at me with her striking eyes, so dark they appeared almost black. "I said, never you mind."

I pulled out one of the chairs set around the table and sat down. From years of experience, I knew it was no use talking to her, not until she'd finished the spell. She reached behind her to the tall, built-in shelves and took down a wooden bowl. Slowly, with precision, she began to put in bits of the plants and herbs, some earth, three of the twigs — arranged in a triangle — and then more earth and topped it off with the three hairs.

I'd seen her do this before. It was some kind of curse or something. Something she'd warned me over and over I was way too young to attempt yet. Being ten, I felt my knowledge was vast already. It was hard to believe I still had more to learn.

Little hairs stood on end at the back of my neck when

she waved her hand over the bowl. I could almost see the friction in the air snap to attention. She reached for the black candle burning brightly in the middle of the table and tipped it over the bowl. The flame danced precariously while she dripped three drops of wax onto her mixture.

"Fallay, amere, asitoy, deviene!"

I knew the words. I whispered them now as she spoke them, adding my power to hers. Suddenly, the bowl erupted into a large, white *poof*. It took a moment for the smoke to clear. Once it had, that same glaring face was looking at me again.

"It's finished. Now, tell me," she said. "What have you done?"

# CHAPTER 1

My life was over. I was totally and irrevocably screwed.

My bare toes dangled in the cold water of the small lake nestled deep in the forest. An owl hooted in the distance, and a little animal scurried around in the brush behind me, unconcerned with my fate. Despite being alone in the dark, nature soared all around me. Even the trees stirred, swaying and dancing in the wind. Life continued on regardless of the fact that mine was finished. Try as I might, I could find no solution to my problem.

Starting over wasn't an option. My budding career was finished. Gossip would follow me with deadly talons and kill any chance I had at finding another position. There was no one to get me out of this one. No one to counteract what I had done in haste and anger.

It was Samhain. Halloween. The most powerful day of the year for witches. On top of that, there was a full moon. Even knowing this and all the havoc I could wreak, I had not used discretion. Not by a long shot. No. Instead, I'd allowed myself to be caught up in the moment and had unleashed something vile and angry inside of me that had been brewing for days. Weeks, in fact.

What I had done was bad. Very bad.

Jazel had died five long years ago, and although I'd come close, I hadn't learned all her secrets. I might rant and rave and curse the fates from here to eternity, but I knew that in the end, the blame was mine alone. I'd let my temper get the best of me, and in one stupid moment, I had blown everything.

They'd seen what I had done.

Blair had it coming. There was no doubt about that. She'd poked and tormented me every day over the past two months until it got so bad I couldn't control my temper any longer. And today, of all days, she had been at her worst. Not only with me—dressed as a witch, no less—but with one of my children as well. Little Eva, also dressed as a witch, emulating her new favorite teacher, yours truly. She'd told me this with a shy smile I'd done my best to encourage.

The unfortunate little mite came from the saddest part of town. Dirt poor, her costume had left much to be desired. From her homemade, felt black hat—stapled up the back into a cone—to her ratty, thrift-store cape, all the way to her oversized, scuffed, black boots, she'd managed the most thoughtful and pitiable costume. The other children, led by my example, did their best to give Eva thoughtful, kind encouragement.

It had been a great day until Blair had waltzed into our room. Her sneer had soon turned to a snicker at the sight of little Eva. She'd gone so far as to point and remark, "Gad, I wondered where that smell was coming from. Did you dig those clothes out of a dumpster?"

The room had grown silent until Eva ducked her head in shame and began to cry quietly.

"Get out," I'd said.

With a triumphant smile, Blair whirled around in her fancy, store-bought cape and long, red wig and glided from the room. I'd spent the next hour trying to wipe the terrible scene from my children's minds.

After school, after all the little ones had scurried away in the excitement of tricks and treats, I'd headed for the staff room. Blair was there, with the rest of them, drinking and eating Halloween goodies we'd all brought in. Being a supply teacher, I wasn't actually one of them, but I'd hoped I was creating some semblance of belonging. I'd earned their respect over days of hard work and even harder socializing. And when I'd heard that the teacher I covered for was not returning, I'd been encouraged by many of them to apply for the position.

Now it was all for naught.

In one terrible, unguarded moment of rage, I'd focused

on that loathsome bitch, standing there amidst her minions, and let her have it. "You were unjustifiably cruel to Eva. You have no right to make a child — any child — feel that way."

She waved her hand as though swatting a pest and raised an eyebrow at me. "You take things too personally, *Petal*. If you want to make it as a teacher, you need to thicken your skin."

The others were uncomfortable. I could see it in the way they avoided eye contact with me and fidgeted with their cupcakes and plastic cups of punch.

This bitch needed some serious attention. Not just dumping a coffee on her from across the room or making her trip, or having terrible visions of ants crawling up her arms. That would have been too easy. So, I'd made the ultimate connection.

Eye to eye, I'd held her in my power and brought her down. All the way to the floor onto her hands and knees, her head still frozen in my direction, eye contact never breaking. She hadn't gone gracefully. She'd cried out in fear and confusion of losing control of her own body.

"You should be more careful what you say to me," I'd hissed out. There'd been no mistaking my part in her humility.

Once she regained control of her faculties — and body parts — she'd pointed at me and cried, "Witch!"

God, how I hated that word.

Slowly, everyone in the room had backed away from

me. Some had even pointed, mouths hanging open in fear. What else was there for me to do but run away? Like a coward, I'd rushed through the halls and out the door, not even bothering to retrieve my favorite mug. Good thing I'd left my bag in my car at lunchtime. I'd fled to my rented home, changed out of my costume, and headed out into the thick forest that surrounded me on three sides. The high, broad trees swallowed me up, leaving no trace of my presence.

Now, here I sat, contemplating my dilemma.

How was I to live without a job, a purpose? I loved teaching school. I'd encouraged and molded those young, fertile minds just as Jazel had done with mine. Though I hadn't taught them magic as I'd been taught, I'd given them respect and attention. The brief time we'd had together had been inspiring for me as well. Especially with little Eva.

A hiss sounded from behind, making me jump.

Looking over my shoulder, I slowly got to my feet, my senses suddenly on high alert. My bare toes curled, gripping the rough surface of the flat rock I stood upon. A beam of light flashed through the trees, soon making contact and causing a loud, cracking sound.

What the hell was that?

Frozen to the spot, I could only gape in amazement as a flurry of light beams began errant streaks through the woods, each of them ending in a loud crack against a hard surface. A rustling through the brush gave the impression of someone fleeing. Moments later, silence.

In the small clearing before the lake, a dark shape suddenly emerged. Swinging its gaze around, it soon settled upon me. It was a man, I presumed, by its broad size, and as it drew nearer and then stopped barely twenty feet away, I saw I was correct. He stared at me from his imposing height, viewing me from head to toe, assessing me.

"Hello?" I ventured. My heart pounded, and my skin tingled in warning. This man was dangerous.

He nodded his head once in way of greeting. Grasped in his left hand, lowered against his thigh, was a weapon. Black and white, it appeared to glow. Shaped like a medieval sword, a narrow cylinder ran down the length of the steel blade. The man's hand gripped the elaborate hilt. I assumed this weapon fired laser bolts.

"Hunting for something?" I tried again.

Another nod.

"Did you catch it?"

His head slowly moved from side to side.

"I guess I'll leave you to it then." I eased down to retrieve my socks and shoes. When the man remained rooted to the spot, I began to don them, keeping my eyes on him all the while. "You must be new around here. I haven't seen you in town."

Nothing.

Finished, I stood up and began to walk. I didn't go

toward him. Instead, I walked at an angle, putting more distance between us. His eyes were ever watchful and followed my steps.

As I got to the edge of the forest, he said, "Wait." His voice was deep, with a trace of an accent I couldn't place.

I paused, wanting nothing more than to flee. "Yes?"

He leveled his weapon and fiddled with it before aiming it right at me. Before I could leap into the woods, he fired, allowing me only a split second to raise my hand in defense. I saw a beam of light shoot forth. And then, nothing. Only darkness.

When I awoke, it was to the warm sun shining down on my face. Directly across from my bed, the blind over the bedroom window was up. In my exhaustion last night, I must have forgotten to pull it down. I sat up and swung my legs over the side of the bed, and stretched my arms above my head. For some reason, I had a crick in my neck, and my body felt tender and achy.

The condition of my body wasn't the only thing weighing on me. Something wasn't right. It felt as though doom and gloom had been stitched into a cloak and thrown over my shoulders to rest upon my back. I searched my memory for what could be the cause of my discomfort, and it all came back to me.

Blair. The school staff room. What I had done.

How could I forget my life was over? Actually, I was

surprised the town hadn't formed a posse and came after me with burning torches last night.

I looked down at my feet and noticed my socks. My shoes sat neatly on the floor by the edge of the bed. I was fully dressed. Strange, considering I usually slept naked. The clothes I wore were from yesterday. *Very strange.* I remembered going into the woods to sit by the lake after the fiasco at work. Everything after that was a blank. Eyes closed, I tried to think.

Flashes of light. I remembered that. And yes, a dark shape emerging from the woods. A man, I believe. We'd spoken, hadn't we?

My head began to ache. I got up and changed into a pair of jeans and a long-sleeved cotton shirt. My long hair hung loose down my back, which was unusual for me. I pulled it forward and braided it before tossing it over my shoulder.

In my little kitchen, I put on coffee and made a piece of toast. Breakfast in hand, I decided to sit out on the porch to eat. As soon as I maneuvered the door open, I dropped both items, shattering my second favorite mug.

There, sprawled out, with his shoulders propped up against the rails directly across from me, was a giant dressed all in black leather. Blond, shaggy hair hung to his massive shoulders. His chin was drooped onto a formidable chest. Long, muscular legs stretched out before him with calf-length, black boots on big feet. He appeared to be sleeping from the way his steady, deep breaths made his chest rise and fall. And yet, the remnants of my breakfast strewn around him hadn't stirred him in the least.

# CHAPTER 2

I wasn't sure what to do, so I sidestepped to contemplate him from the relative safety of the stairway. Judging by the size of him, my shabby front door wouldn't keep him out if he was inclined to barge inside. Running into the woods would be my best option of escape. That's if he ever woke up.

The notion that this man meant me harm was hardly unreasonable, considering the fact we were practically out in the middle of nowhere, and he was obviously drunk or on something. Either that, or he was a very deep sleeper, or perhaps he was hurt? Perusing his fine, solid form, he appeared to be unscathed, so what was he doing here?

A sudden thought made my belly lurch. Maybe he was a parent of one of the kids at school or a spouse of one of the teachers? Maybe he'd heard about my little show yesterday and had got himself liquored up and came out here to deal with me? But why had he stopped on the front porch?

The flicker of a memory suddenly entered my head, me

standing at the lake speaking to a man. This man? I couldn't be completely certain. I remembered flashes of light and a weapon—some sort of medieval sword. There didn't appear to be anything like that here.

A bee buzzed around the man's nose, and he raised a heavy hand to wave at the insect. His feet rocked side to side, and his knees bent up. His features winced as he turned his head right to left as though disagreeing with someone, and both shoulders shrugged and rolled. Then one dazzling blue eye squinted open.

I moved down to the first step, preparing to run.

"Wait," he said.

The slight accent in his voice made me pause. I also had the strangest feeling of déjà vu. He began struggling to his feet, using the railing for support. He leaned heavily against the rails and studied me.

"What do you want?" I asked. At the slightest inclination of hostility, I was ready to bolt.

His eyes bore into mine as though they would freeze me in place. "Last night," he began. "Tell me what you remember."

So my faint memory was correct. I had seen him last night.

"Not very much," I admitted. His frown made me want to offer more. "I think I remember speaking to a man, you presumably, out by the lake in the woods. There were flashes of light." Or were there?

He nodded in agreement.

"I remember a sword."

His left hand twitched, and his fingers curled as though to grasp a hilt. He gave a single nod in the affirmative.

"What was going on? What were those lights?"

He exhaled heavily as though it pained him. "I was hunting."

I seemed to recall those words as well. "Hunting what? That obviously wasn't a gun you were using. It looked like laser bolts flying around."

"They were laser bolts. What I hunt is not of this world."

*Hunt*—present tense. He hadn't killed it then. I suppose his words should have shocked me. If not the truth of them, then the fear that he was deranged in believing them. I'd seen many things. Terrible, frightening things that I would not describe as being of this world. And yet, I had the feeling he spoke of something else.

"You do not seem surprised." A statement, not an accusation.

I shrugged. "I've seen a lot of bizarre stuff in my life."

He could have laughed at my boast, but he didn't. Instead, his tongue stole out to moisten his bottom lip. "Could I trouble you for a drink of water?"

That little request would require me to pass him and

enter the house, thereby leaving me vulnerable. "There's a well over there." I gestured with a turn of my head at a spot to the right of me. His gaze obligingly steered in that direction.

I backed down the remainder of the steps and gave him ample space to move past me. He took the steps two at a time, and his long strides ate up the yard. It took him a moment to figure out that he had to maneuver the arm of the pump up and down to draw forth the water. An old tin cup lay in the tall grass, which he plucked up and placed below the trickle that soon became a steady flow. When he lifted the cup to his lips and drank deeply, I cringed. The water was fresh and clean, but I couldn't say the same about the cup.

The giant drank four cupfuls before he dropped it to the grass and used the back of his arm to wipe his mouth. Then he turned his attention to me again. "I need to continue tracking. I would appreciate the return of my weapon."

His strange accent caught me off guard. "Wait. What? You're asking me for your laser bolt sword thingy?"

He nodded.

"What makes you think I have it?" I'd know if I did, wouldn't I?

He strode forward, not close enough to make me run off, but enough to make me nervous. "Because you took it from me last night."

"How could I take your weapon if you had it?" Guess he'd failed to notice that he was at least a foot taller than me and probably weighed twice as much as I did. A sudden vision popped into my head. "Wait a second. I remember you raising that sword and aiming it right at me," I accused.

He didn't argue, just nodded in confirmation. *Ass.*

"A laser bolt flew out at me. I only had time to raise my arm in defense." I'm amazed I wasn't charred to a crisp right now. And he had the audacity to accuse me of taking his weapon?

He crept a little closer. "Right."

How ridiculous. "And?" There had to be more to the story.

His giant chest rose and fell with a heavy sigh. "You raised your hand and sent the bolt back at me, knocking me to the ground."

"I did?" *Impressive.*

"Then you stormed over and ripped the weapon from my hands."

"Wow. Then what did I do?"

He gestured toward the house. "Went home, I'm presuming. I tracked you back here, barely having the strength to make it up the steps before collapsing."

I bit back the retort that if I hadn't turned the tide, his indisposition would have been mine. He'd only been stunned, at least, not charred, but that didn't excuse his intent. "So, it must be inside?" If what he said was true and not some fabricated fairy tale.

A blood-chilling cry of what I assumed to be an animal sounded from the woods close by where we stood. Both of us stared into the dark depth of the thick trees then back at each other.

"Would you mind fetching it?" he asked.

Dumbly, I nodded. Another scream and the loud rustling of brush had my companion mouthing the word *hurry* to me.

Without another word, I scrambled up the steps and into the house to search.

I found the weapon under my bed. Grabbing hold of the thing, I rushed back outside and practically threw it into his waiting hands. We stood side by side, our backs ramrod straight, staring at the line of trees. Waiting.

"Get ready," he said, fiddling with the settings on the weapon.

"Those who are about to die...." I couldn't help but mutter.

"Not today."

In a blur, a thing twice the size of a bear and black as coal barreled from the woods and charged at us on its powerful hind legs. Raising the sword, my companion volleyed off shot after shot. The beast, wily and wicked, dodged side to side, never losing stride, hardly noticing the shots that grazed its mangy fur and sizzled like water thrown on hot ash.

Seeing there was no hope, I prepared to bolt. First, I

made eye contact with the giant. The look he shot me was grim. Seeing my intent to flee, he gave a nod in assent before turning his attention back to the beast. Less than fifty feet away, I was given a full view of its hideous visage. A snarling jaw revealed long, pointy, white teeth, the spray of saliva making its face slick and slimy. Long, hairy arms tipped with hooked claws stroked the air, drawing it ever closer to our proximity.

"Run!" I hollered, making a break for the house.

Watching him over my shoulder, I could see my plea fell on stubborn ears. He'd given up the laser show and now held his sword ready for old-fashioned battle. Halfway to the porch, I turned again and saw the beast had slowed and soon came to rest scant feet from the man. While both stared each other down, I bent and sunk my fingers into the tall grass and dug at the earth, gathering a handful of dirt. The beast agilely moved back and forth and side to side, bare inches from the lethal sword that thrust and swung in mighty arcs.

Closing my eyes for a second, I waved my left hand methodically over my head. The chirp of a sparrow greeted me. Opening my eyes, I waited while a single feather floated to the ground. I reached to lift it. Slowly, I moved toward the pair, now growling in earnest at each other. As I walked, I held my right hand out straight and then, using my left fingers, pushed the feather into the dirt in my palm. Though much closer to the duo, neither seemed to note my presence.

"Calaben, satrine, manet, and doone." This spell was easy. Child's play, really, when you wanted to gentle or subdue a wild animal. Judging by the size of the beast, I worried I might need a wagonload of dirt and an entire bird.

The giant finally caught sight of me. "Get out of here," he snapped.

I ignored him and leveled my gaze on my target. "Lenis, malacus, suavis." Ancient language, I remember having a bitch of a time perfecting, now came easily to me. Jazel had told me I had a natural affinity to nature and to call upon it when casting spells. My power on its own was potent. The combination of the words and the power of the earth amped it up considerably.

Before my eyes, I watched the wild beast transform. Its physical attributes remained unchanged. The character, however, visibly shifted. The snarling mouth closed, and the clawed limbs dropped down to its furry sides. The massive head lowered submissively, and it sat back on its haunches. The long, thin tail I'd failed to notice earlier actually swayed back and forth across the grass.

The giant lowered the sword and stared at me, his mouth hanging open slightly. "What the hell?" he finally said.

I shrugged, dropped the dirt, and brushed off my hands. "A spell to subdue the wild," I explained. "What is this thing?"

"A Kedago. Deadlier than anything you'd find here."

"Here? As in this town?"

The drilling look I got made me shiver. "As in this planet."

He reached out suddenly and pushed me out of the way, forcibly enough to send me sprawling. By the time I got to my feet, he'd swung the sword in a great arc and brought it down to cut off the beast's head.

"Holy shit, you son of a bitch." I couldn't believe it. As I stared in dismay at the carnage before me, the thing began to disintegrate. It took about a full minute, but soon it was completely gone. I spun on the giant. "Why? You didn't have to do that."

"How long did you think you could hold it? Even if you could manage the beast, what would you do with it? Keep it?"

True, I'd always wanted a pet, but I was thinking more along the lines of a cat—black, of course.

The giant gestured over his shoulder in the direction of the road. "Besides, I think you have enough to worry about right now."

I'd been so caught up in the beast drama that I'd failed to hear what sounded like a mini-caravan coming down the dirt road toward my house. I was far off the beaten path, and not many cars came down this way. They must be coming for me. I suddenly pictured an old-fashioned witch burning.

"Damn." I glared at the giant and turned to bolt for the

house.

Taking the stairs two at a time, I rushed through the door and strode into my room. My suitcase was in the closet. I yanked it down and tossed it open on the bed. Grabbing an armload of hanging clothes, I dumped them in the case and bent down to snatch up several pairs of shoes, cursing myself all the while. I had intended to pack up and be off first thing this morning.

I heard my front door bang shut and held my breath until the giant poked his head into my room. "Get out," I told him.

"I would think you'd want my help."

"I don't want anything from you." I didn't want to even try and contemplate what had just taken place and all the implications it entailed.

I turned my attention back to my packing. I tossed a bunch of stuff into a toiletry bag and began pulling out drawers of my dresser. There was so much I needed to take, and I wasn't sure if I'd get the chance to sneak back and get the rest.

"Forget all that. Let's go," he said.

"Easy for you to say. I need this stuff. I can't just leave with nothing." I shoved some socks and panties, along with the toiletry bag, into the suitcase, flipped over the top, and held it down with one hand while I zipped it up with the other.

"They're here." The giant had moved across the room to look out the window that faced the front of the house.

"Damn it." I joined him and saw four cars move down the driveway and block in my car, not bothering to mind the grass.

"What exactly did you do?"

I shrugged. "Had a little meltdown at school yesterday. In front of witnesses."

The giant whistled low. "Got a back door?"

"Yeah."

He gripped his sword in one hand and took my suitcase with the other. I had no choice but to rush with him through the house and outside. Then we were barreling toward the woods, the sounds of an angry mob clamoring for my blood behind us.

# CHAPTER 3

Once the giant and I reached the safety of the trees, we circled around to spy on the mob. About ten people were spread out on my lawn. One of them was Blair, who had a big, burly guy standing next to her, probably her husband or brother. I recognized a couple of other teachers from the school. They peered around nervously, and I got the impression they'd rather be anywhere else. The rest of the group was mostly men I didn't know or barely knew from around town. A few of them sported shotguns. One of the men pounded on my front door so loud that I felt my teeth rattle. Two patrol cars pulled up the driveway next.

"Wow, you really messed up," the giant said.

I nodded once and swallowed hard. I'd entertained the potential but hadn't actually expected them to come at me with such force.

"Maybe I should have waited to kill the Kedago."

It would have been a good distraction, but no doubt

something else they'd hold me responsible for, fueling their fury. "Hopefully, when they realize I'm gone, they'll leave. Then I can get the rest of my stuff and my car and go."

"Go where?"

"I'll figure it out."

We watched them mull about for a while. The policemen went up to the door and disappeared inside.

"I wonder if you can get arrested for witchcraft," I mumbled. No doubt Blair would call it assault. She'd probably get away with it, too, considering the witnesses.

"If authorities are involved, you won't be safe anywhere," he informed me.

"Thanks for the vote of confidence."

When the police came outside, the group shifted their sights to the tree line. The cops began waving their arms around and pointing in different directions.

"They're dividing into groups and going to search," he said.

"You think?"

I didn't know what to do. The woods were vast. I could probably hide out in them, but for how long was anyone's guess. Staying here wasn't an option. One of the female teachers and a big guy with a gun settled in on the porch, so I couldn't hope to get back inside.

I began striding through the woods. When I heard the heavy footsteps of my companion, I stopped and reached out my hand. "You can give me back my bag now, thanks."

He stopped walking and stared at me. "What are you planning?"

I shrugged. "Not sure yet. Whatever I do, it won't involve you."

"I can't just abandon you," he insisted.

"I'm not your problem, okay? Seriously, you should get as far away from me as possible." I gestured for my case again, but he shook his head. "Dude, really?" When he stared at me stubbornly, I gave him a nasty look. "Fine. Keep it, then. It'll only slow me down anyway."

I turned and began to stalk deeper into the forest. I heard the giant's steps fall into line behind me.

"What's your name?" If I decided to curse him out later, I'd like to make it personal.

"Rein," he said.

"Seriously? Like from a cloud?"

"No, like in use restraint or a bridle on a horse. What's your name?"

"Petal."

"Um-hum."

"Really. My parents were a little weird. If I'd been a boy, they said they would've called me River or Laker."

"Real nature lovers."

"Exactly."

"Can you go to them now? If they're anything like you,

they should be able to protect you."

A flash of pain shot through me. "No. They're dead." They'd died in a small plane crash the year before Jazel passed away. As for being like me, they weren't.

The sound of crunching boots and a pair of male voices made me quicken my pace.

"That witch is long gone," I heard one of the men say.

"Then why'd she leave her car?" the other asked.

"Maybe she took her broom," the first one replied, then barked with laughter.

"Idiots," I hissed.

Rein came up beside me and veered me off to the right. "This way."

"I know these woods, and there's nothing up that way. If we go straight, we'll hit a stream we can follow to some caves. At least it's shelter." When I went to shift my direction, he pulled me back to the right again.

"I came in this way. My transportation isn't far."

"Your transportation? You have an ATV?" No way could a car get through here.

"Something like that."

I allowed him to lead us through the forest, taking us deeper and deeper until I could no longer make out the sounds of pursuit. He'd gotten ahead of me, and I watched him from the back. I had to admit he was attractive. His immense size made me feel all small and delicate. Pure masculinity emanated from him, igniting my female hormones. It wasn't just his obscene height, but the strength and confidence he radiated turned my knees to jelly. Not to mention he was mysterious — something I'd always found incredibly irresistible. His hair was so blond it was almost white, in stark contrast to the black leather he wore. Tight pants fit him like a second skin, showing off long, muscular legs and a tight, rock-hard ass.

Despite the awesome view he presented, I had to remind myself I was following a virtual stranger into the deep, dark depths of the forest. I shook my head. Perhaps I wasn't the only sorceress in the woods?

Something Rein had said during all that chaos earlier gnawed at the corner of my mind. "What did you call that thing? A Kedago?"

"Yeah," he answered over his shoulder. He slowed his pace, and I came up nearly to his side.

"You said it wasn't from this world. What exactly did you mean by that?" Even without touching him, I could feel his sudden tension. Guess I hit a nerve.

"That's what I said?" He laughed a little. "Heat of the moment and all that."

I didn't buy it. "You seemed pretty sure."

"You saw it. Have you ever seen anything like that before? Looked out of this world to me. Maybe it was a Sasquatch or Bigfoot, or whatever they call them around here."

"You were hunting it. And you know what it's called. How do you know that?"

He shrugged.

"So you're a monster hunter?" I gestured to the sword at his side.

"I have an interest in strange beasts. Let's leave it at that."

"And do you happen to run into a lot of strange beasts?"

"You could say that."

"Do you work for the government or something?" That might make sense.

"No."

He stalked ahead again to avoid my questions, so I slowed and then stopped altogether. He'd been elusive with his answers, and now he was leading me to his *transportation.* When he kept on, I veered to the left. No one was following me anymore. The men who'd been in the woods must have given up or gone in another direction.

It wasn't like I needed Rein for protection. If I put my mind and efforts into it, I could cloak my presence or, if it came down to it, scare my pursuers off. Earlier I'd been a little freaked out, and then I kind of panicked and lacked the time to do any spells. Dealing with one oversized, wild beast in the heat of the moment had been one thing. Dealing with a dozen angry human beings was quite another.

It didn't take long to hear the approaching steps behind

me. Even before I turned around, I knew it was Rein. I didn't get the chance to tell him to buzz off. Instead, just as I stopped and was about to turn, I felt something hit me in the back of the head hard enough to send me to my knees.

Ears ringing, I leaned forward and dug my hands beneath the carpet of dried, crinkling leaves of seasons past, anxious to connect with the soil. Before I could draw power from the earth, something hit me again, this time making me fall forward flat onto my belly. A black pair of boots appeared within my line of sight right before everything went black.

# CHAPTER 4

When I awoke, my head felt fuzzy, and my tongue felt like I'd spent the last hour licking a cardboard box. It took me a moment to orient myself and realize my hands were strapped to the armrests of a high-back chair. It was identical to the one beside me where Rein was seated.

I licked my lips before I confronted him. "You shot me?"

He wouldn't meet my gaze. "You gave me no choice."

His profile irritated me, so I turned my head forward to stare at what looked to be the front windshield of a car. I must have been out for a while since everything appeared dark. I couldn't figure out what all those white specs were, so I squeezed my eyes shut and opened them several times. The view remained unchanged. It soon registered those were stars I was seeing.

I swung my gaze around, taking in everything. The control panel before me was high-tech, extending around the sides of the interior space and overhead. Not something you'd find in an automobile—more like a small plane. Rein wasn't steering with a wheel; it resembled an old-fashioned gamer joystick.

"What's going on?" I flexed my hands, noting the restraints weren't overly tight but secure enough to hold me immobile. When he sat there all tight-lipped, I tried again. "Are you kidnapping me?"

"No, of course not."

"Then, what the hell?"

So his transportation was a plane. It obviously wasn't a helicopter. I'd flown once before but in a huge 747. My view from the tiny window had been pretty bleak, considering it had been a night flight. I didn't recall the stars or darkness being so encompassing.

I leaned forward a fraction to attempt a better look, trying to gauge how high up we were. Something glowing off in the distance to my far right caught my attention. I squeezed my eyes shut.

"Are there side effects to that blast you gave me?" I opened my eyes and turned an imploring gaze on my companion.

"No. You should be fine now," he informed me.

"You did something to my head or my vision."

He stared at me, assessing. "There's nothing wrong with you."

I gestured with my head to my right. "Then why the hell am I looking at Saturn?"

"Shit. Saturn?" He leaned forward and peered around me. "Damn, we're making good time."

"Good time?" I sputtered. "Are we in space? Outer freaking space? Am I on a spaceship?"

"Yes. Don't start screaming."

"That's all you have to say? Don't start screaming? Are you kidding me?"

My body felt cold and hot at the same time. My vision blurred for a second, and I thought I might actually faint. I'd never fainted in my life. After all the bone-chilling things I'd seen, including that bloody Kedago, I'd never felt inclined to faint. There was no way I'd do it now.

*Concentrate!*

I had to get a hold of myself. First, I started with deep breaths and wiggling my toes, getting the blood flowing. The view out the window did nothing but reinforce my panic, so I focused on Rein instead.

"Why are we in space?"

"Fastest way to get to where we're going," he replied.

"And where are we going?"

"Someplace safe." He pointed straight ahead. "That way."

Why was he being such an asshole? Annoyance battled with my fear. "Holy shit, I can't believe this is happening to me. Do you even know where you're headed?"

He stared at me like I was a dolt. "Of course I do."

"Then why won't you tell me?"

"I just did."

When he lifted his arm, I cut him off. "If you point again, I'm going to start screaming."

He dropped his hand into his lap and frowned. "You don't need to get upset."

My gaze went from him to my secured wrists and back to him again. "You have me tied up in a friggin' spaceship against my will," I reminded him.

"Would you rather be back there? On the run from a mob of witch hunters?"

I wasn't sure which was worse. "Back there, I was at least getting away from crazy. Now I'm trapped sitting right next to it."

He appeared offended. "I'm not crazy. And I'm not dangerous. You have nothing to fear from me."

"Said the freak who shot, kidnapped, tied me up, and took me into outer space." If it sounded sarcastic, so be it.

"Some thank you this is," he muttered.

"Thank you? You expect me to thank you?"

"They might have killed you back there," he said.

I snorted. "I doubt it. Arrested me, maybe. For assault. That's all they could get on me. No matter how many witnesses there were, the cops would never charge me with witchcraft. I don't know where you come from, but that's not how we deal with things on my planet."

"Um-hum."

They had seen what I'd done. But they were logically thinking adults. After processing it in their minds, they'd no doubt convinced themselves it was a trick. Although, they had come after me in full force. That part was strange. Why not just send in a couple of cops?

"Do you think any of them saw that thing? The Kedago? Do you think they believed I had something to do with it?" It could explain their overreaction. From the conversation I'd overheard between those two men in the woods, I knew they were looking for me. I couldn't hope to think they were only searching for the beast.

He shrugged. "I don't know. Anything is possible."

"All of this is so messed up. First the fiasco at school, then the light show in the woods, then waking up and finding you on my porch and me not knowing how I got home."

"I tried to explain that," he said.

I ignored him. "Then the battle with the beast. Then the mob. Now, this."

"Chalk it up to a bad day. Or a bad couple of days."

I shook my head to clear my fuzzy brain. Maybe it was the altitude, but I started feeling dizzy again. I decided to stop processing stuff and turn my attention to him. "You said you were a monster hunter?"

He gave a quick nod.

"Do you consider me a monster?"

"What? No. Why would you think I believe—"

"Because of what you saw me do. First with your weapon and then with the Kedago."

His eyes bore into mine for a moment too long, and I knew I was right. Fear enveloped me again. "Are you going to kill me?"

"No." He turned his gaze back to the view. "You were in trouble back there. And despite what you said, I don't think you could have handled it. You're too valuable to leave to that mob."

"Should I be flattered?"

"I think it's in both of our interests if you stay with me a while. You've proven yourself to be an asset. I think we should combine forces."

"Combine forces? To do what?" I thought for a moment. "You hunt monsters. I'm beginning to think your efforts aren't solely concentrated on Earth."

"Correct."

"So there are monsters all over the galaxy?"

He nodded.

"And you hunt them?" After another nod, I asked, "Why?"

He ran a hand over his eyes and massaged his temple with his fingers as though he battled exhaustion or a headache.

Or both. "It's not a matter of wanting to do it. It's of having to do it."

"I don't understand."

"It's confusing as hell. Look, right now, we're in a spaceship, okay?"

I nodded.

"I had to fly to Earth to hunt that thing. It wasn't the first time, and it won't be the last. Things escape from other worlds, and I'm part of a task force charged with tracking them down."

I wasn't sure what to say. "Okay." But then, something occurred to me. "You needed a ship to get to Earth. But how did the Kedago get there? I can't believe that thing has the intelligence to fly."

"It didn't need a ship."

"So the obvious question is how did it get there?"

He contemplated the view for over a minute before he answered me. "There are some instances of havoc-wreakers that deliberately bring species to other planets to intentionally cause trouble, though sometimes it's unintentional. Things sneak aboard ships, just like creatures on Earth will catch a ride on cars or trains or planes. But then there are times when gateways open up, and things sometimes slip through."

"What?" I could wrap my head around creatures getting there by spaceship, intentionally or unintentionally, as crazy as this whole thing seemed. But gateways?

"Take Earth, for example. On certain days, like the summer and winter solstice, or when there's a blue moon, or the planets align, or sometimes even during a full moon, or a tornado, or other weather phenomenon, it's hard to predict, things happen causing a thinning or rift in the space-time continuum. During that time, things have been known to slip through."

"It was Samhain. Halloween. And there was a full moon. Is that why the Kedago got through?" I'd hate to think it had been roaming around longer than that.

"Most likely, yes."

I shifted in my seat to get more comfortable. "I'm not going anywhere. Can you please release me?"

He narrowed his eyes, contemplating me for a moment. Then he reached down and pulled a long, thin knife from his boot. I held my breath while he continued to hold my gaze.

"I only strapped you in so you wouldn't fling out of your seat during take-off. It can get a little rough."

"Isn't that what the seatbelt's for?"

Ignoring my question, he cut loose the binding on the wrist closest to him. He paused a moment. "I also couldn't take the chance you'd become hysterical when you woke up. If you push one wrong button in here, I might not be able to correct the mistake in time. The ship could go down, and we both could die."

I nodded, acknowledging his warning.

He had to reach over me to free my other wrist. His arm pushed against my breasts as he began to saw at the rope. The jolt of heat I experienced from his touch surprised me. Judging by the tense, determined look on his face, I wasn't the only one who felt it. The task seemed to take him twice as long this time. Whether it was intentional or not, I had to wonder.

He finished cutting, and as he moved away, his hair brushed my face. I inhaled his masculine sent, a mixture of pine and something else I couldn't quite pinpoint but found exceptionally erotic. I watched him settle back into his seat, tuck his knife away, and reach for the control arm. What was it about him that intrigued me so?

*Danger.*

Ah, yes. That was probably it.

We continued to soar through the starry night sky. I could have almost enjoyed the light show if it weren't for the fact that every minute spent on this ship took me farther and farther from Earth.

I filled the void with conversation. As difficult as it was grasping the idea of aliens and monsters, I suppose being a supernatural-being myself made the concept easier to accept. However, the idea of gateways was foreign to me.

"So what do you have in mind? For us, I mean."

He shrugged.

"You must have a plan? Us teaming up? That's what

you said. Do you want me to help you hunt?" The set of his jaw made me think I might possibly have bruised his male ego. "It's okay to admit you need help."

"I don't need your help," he insisted.

Yep, definitely wounded.

"I said the arrangement could be beneficial to us both. You get rescued from the mob, and in the meantime, until things cool off, you won't be a complete burden to me. You get to earn your keep."

If that's the way he needed to spin it, then fine. "About these gateways to Earth…I have to admit the idea really freaks me out."

"What do you want to know?"

I thought for a moment. "Everything," I decided. "Where are they? How do they work? Are they linked to just one other planet? Do they go both ways?" I could have gone on and on, but I paused when Rein held up his hand.

"One question at a time." He fiddled with the control arm to sashay around what looked like a huge boulder looming too close for comfort. The scenery reinforced the fact of where I was and what I was doing. As much as I wanted answers about gateways, another flock of questions bubbled up.

"Where are we going? And how long will we be gone?"

"Curious little thing, aren't you?"

I narrowed my gaze at him. "If our positions were

reversed, I'm sure you'd have a lot of questions for me as well. I mean, I don't even know you. One minute I'm sitting on a rock contemplating my future, the next minute, you're trying to zap me with a laser bolt. Which, by the way, was completely unprovoked."

He exhaled loudly. "I only planned on knocking you unconscious. When you woke up, you would have figured what you'd seen was a dream."

"Well, pardon me for defending myself."

He had the audacity to wink at me. "If you hadn't, then I wouldn't be sitting here right now enjoying your delightful company."

I arched a brow at his sarcasm. I had to admit he was correct. If things had gone differently, I could be tied to a stake atop a pile of kindling. Instead, I was kidnapped by an alien and flying through outer space in a spaceship to God knew where.

Some choice.

# CHAPTER 5

"Now's a good time to return to Kameri and check the gate. Something must have happened," Rein informed me. "Despite the thinning of the veil that I mentioned, there are safeguards in place to prevent things from slipping through."

"What kind of safeguards?"

"Like a lock," he said. "The gate on Kameri must have been tampered with."

"Is that where the Kedago came from?"

"Yes."

I wasn't sure how I felt about this, our first mission together. I'd seen that beast up close and personal, and I could only imagine the hellish place it came from. "Is it safe?"

"No planet is completely safe. At least none that I've seen. Kameri is small and wild. Mainly inhabited by beasts."

"No people?"

He shrugged. "I've yet to see any."

A big ball of blue and green soon came into view. "Is

that it?"

Rein nodded. He guided the ship toward a large, green patch. "Hold on."

The pressure of entering the atmosphere reminded me of the rapid, bone-rattling descent of a roller-coaster. I gripped the armrests, held my breath, and tried to not bite my tongue with my clacking teeth. After the force leveled off, I took slow, even breaths, waiting for my belly to come down out of my rib cage.

The view was breathtaking. As the ship swooped toward the surface, I saw huge areas of land and even larger bodies of water. Soon I could make out rocky hills, fields, streams and little lakes dotted around large forests. The trees were like those in Earth's oldest woodlands, being huge and high, the leaves the size of compact cars or with needles the size of swords. There weren't any visible man-made structures.

"It's a lot like old Earth," I said. I'd seen renditions on television and in books.

"Yes. Although about a fifth of the size." He brought us in for a landing in a clearing and unhooked his seatbelt after the ship settled. I unhooked mine as well and got to my feet to follow him into the belly of the ship.

"Can we breathe out there?" A couple of jumpsuits with what looked like gas masks hung on hooks attached to the ship's wall.

"Yeah. The only difference you'll notice, besides the air

being thicker and fresher, is the gravitational pull. Your body will feel about twenty or thirty pounds lighter."

Well, that was a plus.

He pulled on a shoulder harness that held his sword and grabbed a black bag before pressing a green button on the wall, making the door swish up. Putting his hand on the doorframe, he leaned out and cast an assessing gaze around.

"All clear," he said, and jumped down. He swung the bag he held onto his back and held out a hand to me.

"Don't I get a weapon?"

"No."

As I continued to hesitate, he waved an impatient hand at me.

A loud roar of a beast rumbled, making me search the surrounding forest with trepidation. "What if something happens to you?" I asked.

"It won't," he replied, still waving.

"Oh, all right." I took his hand and jumped down.

He let go of me and pushed on a little black triangle, which appeared to be part of a design on the outside of the ship. The door swished shut. "Remember where that is," he told me.

"Fat lot of good it'll do me since I can't fly the ship."

"If anything happens, you'll be safe inside until I return."

"*If* you return," I emphasized.

His lip lifted at the corner, reminding me of an Elvis impersonator. "You worry too much." He peered upward and stretched out his arm toward the sky. "We have about an hour or so of daylight remaining. Should give me enough time to fix the gate and be on our way before night." He began to walk, and I followed him.

"What happens at night?" The way he'd said it made it seem like time was of the essence.

"It gets dark."

"Ha-ha. You're an asshole, you know? Anyone ever tell you that?" Another loud roar, followed by squeals of what sounded like a hundred wild boars, echoed around us.

"All the time."

We wound through the colossal trees, listening to the hum of giant insects and the flapping of what I hoped were birds. When we started walking on what appeared to be a pathway, I asked him about it.

"It's formed by creatures that look like a cross between a sloth and an alligator."

I conjured up a visual in my mind and shuddered. Passing a swamp, I caught sight of a frog-like creature the size of a small dog with wiry hair and the leg of something dangling out of its mouth. Giant daisies with serrated leaves bobbed their heads malevolently.

Despite the surrounding weirdness, I felt a spring in my step, thanks to the lesser gravitational pull, which I quite enjoyed. We moved quickly, and I took comfort in the fact that if we were pursued by anything noxious, we would likely have no trouble outdistancing it.

Just as the light began to dim, we came upon the gateway.

"Here it is," Rein said, pointing at a rock face on the side of a hill off to the right of the trail. Everything around us was moss-covered. The past few minutes had been slick-walking since the green, cushy stuff covered most of the fist-sized rocks in our path.

My curiosity aroused, I took a closer look at the mysterious passageway between worlds. A triangular-shaped gash in the rock served as an entranceway to a pitch-black interior.

"That's it?" I'd been expecting some great, glowing edifice, like something out of *Stargate*.

"That's it," Rein confirmed.

Not large by any means, I wasn't concerned the roaring beast out there would be able to get through. But it was big enough to allow a Kedago passage if it wiggled itself just right.

"Should it be covered or something?" I asked.

Rein reached down and plucked a green, pulsing stone from the corner of the triangle. "There should be another crystal." He gestured to the tip of the gate where an identical one sat in a niche in the stone. "Like these. See if you can find the third." He replaced the crystal, and his gaze scanned the forest floor.

"Figures it'd be green. Good luck finding it in this moss." The black interior of the gateway held me spellbound. Earth was on the other side. All it would take was a few steps…

"Don't." Rein's stern warning jolted me.

"What?"

He came up beside me and stared at me hard. "I know what you're thinking. Just don't."

"I wasn't thinking anything," I lied.

He reached out and gripped my wrist. "You believe you can walk through there and go home. That's not going to happen."

I yanked my wrist, but he held tight. "Maybe the thought did cross my mind. So what? If the Kedago got through, the other side must be in the town I was in. Why did we fly all the way here and not just find the gate on Earth?"

"Think about it. I come through and fix the portal. How do I get back if it's sealed? I'd be trapped here."

He had a point.

"Not only that. There's no guarantee this will go to where it led earlier."

I was still working on problem number one. "Why couldn't you step through and set up the crystals from the inside of the gate?"

"The moment you step through, you're gone. There'd be no time."

Well, shit. There went that idea. "Okay then, the other thing you said. What do you mean? It's not anchored to one place?" He'd said *there's no guarantee*, so there could be a chance.

"No, it's not. Remember what I told you about the solstice and full moon and blue moon?"

"It won't work if it's not the right date?" It'd been a full moon on Halloween the last time it linked to my town. Unless I wanted to wait a very long time, returning in the spaceship would be my best bet.

"Yes."

"But it still goes directly to Earth? You're just not sure where?"

"Yes." His grip tightened as he looked up at the darkening sky. "We're running out of time. I can answer your questions back on the ship. Let's find the last crystal and get out of here."

The edge in his voice halted my interrogation. I nodded and looked pointedly at our hands. After a warning stare, he released me. We both got busy scouring the ground.

Just as I'd begun to lose hope and the land became increasingly dark, a faint pulse of light beneath a mossy log that arched up slightly in the center caught my attention. I walked over and bent down to pick it up. I held it up and called to Rein, "Hey, is this it?"

"Oh, good," he said with obvious relief. Coming up to me, he held out his hand, and I passed him the crystal. "Yeah, this is it."

He wasn't the only one growing anxious. The surrounding roars, growls, snorts, and squeals intensified with the darkness. We strode toward the gate, and I waited while Rein put it into place. A *zing* sounded as all three stones reached out to one another with a light beam.

"How do you think it came loose?" I asked.

He shrugged. "Bad storm might have knocked it, or maybe some animal tried to scurry away with it."

"Does this happen a lot?"

"No, not a lot."

"Well, that's a relief, considering the consequences."

Rein moved toward the path, and I followed him. Our pace was swift.

"What about the gates on Earth? I assume there are safeguards set in place there also, but do you have a problem with people or animals getting through and winding up on other planets?"

"Yeah, that happens as well."

"What happens to the people? Do you have to fetch them and take them home?"

His back was to me since the trail had grown narrow, and we couldn't walk side by side. I had to admire the fine, firm shape of him. Even in the dimming light, he was easy on the eyes.

"There's another task force that deals with Earthlings getting through. It's not very large since most humans are dead by the time they're recovered."

"Dead?" That was a sobering thought.

"Yes. Due to many things. Non-compatible atmosphere. Coming up in water or the middle of a desert. Attacked by wildlife or hostile inhabitants."

"The ones the task force does save, what happens to them? Aren't they afraid they'll talk? Tell the world about what happened to them?"

"They are strictly warned not to speak of it. Some listen, some don't. You see how they're judged on your planet. They're considered insane. And if they try to repeat the process, they can't since the gate's defenses have been reactivated by the task force."

"And if the person discovers a way to deactivate it?"

He shrugged. "Not many instances of that happening. They usually learn their lesson the first time."

I pondered his words while keeping a close eye on our surroundings. What I had first thought were large, black clouds moving overhead soon took the shape of giant birds resembling pterodactyls. Their screams were ungodly and made Rein and I both walk faster.

When the ship came into view, I sighed with relief. As

we moved closer to the craft, Rein put out his arm, nearly clotheslining me.

"Whoa! What's the matter?"

He stood stock-still except for the methodical movement of dropping his bag and reaching for his sword. "Take cover over there." He nodded in the direction of the forest.

"I don't see anything," I insisted.

"Just do it," he hissed.

As I took up position behind a tree, my skin began to tingle with warning. *A little late for that.* I was annoyed with myself. If there was danger lurking, I was usually aware of the threat long before anyone else.

Rein stood facing the ship. Sword drawn. Battle stance.

My scalp heated up, and I caught sight of the tendrils of my hair dancing. And yet, there was no breeze. Even the menagerie had grown eerily silent.

The land was now only lit by the light of the large, full moon. A dark shape flew overhead, casting a faint shadow. Closer now, it no longer reminded me of a prehistoric bird. More of a dragon.

A shower of sparks shot from the creature's nose as it circled around, a precursor to the blast of fire it aimed at the ground from its mouth. Rein reared back as the ship became engulfed in the flames. It quickly heated up and glowed bright red. The creature swung up and flew off, only to make a wide arc and return again.

I stepped from behind the tree. "Rein, run!"

He stared at the ship, which was now seared black. "Son of a bitch! Mother f—"

"Run!" Why wouldn't he listen to me? It'd been the same as with the Kedago. Stubborn, bullheaded dolt.

Just as the creature lowered and opened its mouth to fire again, Rein gained his senses. A trail of flames raced toward him, sparking his bag on fire and making him turn and flee in the opposite direction. He kept up his colorful tirade.

The flames moved faster than his running feet. He wasn't going to make it.

As he tore past me, I moved sideways into the line of fire. I didn't consider the danger, just threw out my hands, palms faced out, and pictured a brick wall, high and strong. The fire stopped right in front of me and reared up like a tidal wave. I pulled my hands back slightly, then pushed them forward, making the flames turn back on themselves and retreat to the source.

The dragon, hovering overhead, shrieked as a fireball rose just below the talons of its feet. It arched, and I swear it contemplated me before it turned and flew away, screaming its ire.

Rein appeared beside me. "Yeah, that's right, bitch. Run!" His fist pumped the air a couple of times.

My hands dropped. We stared at the charred ground

and the blackened ship. There was no way we'd be able to fly to Earth, or anywhere else, in it now.

Whether Rein liked it or not, we'd have to take our chances with the gate.

# CHAPTER 6

Rein quickly got over the fact that I'd saved him. He scowled as he stared at the wreck of his ship.

"We have no choice," I informed him. "We'll have to use the gate. The ship is fried."

He sheathed his sword and ran an arm across his forehead. "God damn it. This entire journey was a complete failure."

"Don't beat yourself up over it. What's done is done." Personally, I was quite pleased with the way things had worked out. I'd wanted to use the gate, to begin with, and go directly back to Earth. Zooming around battling intergalactic monsters was Rein's deal, not mine.

After a few more mutterings, he began walking. I fell into line behind him, latching onto the back of his vest to keep from stumbling in the dark. He reached into his pocket and fumbled around. Moments later, a glow emanated from a circular disk in the palm of his hand and lit a steady beam ahead.

"This is the worst possible scenario," he said.

"I think us being on the ship when it burned would be worse."

"If we'd been five minutes faster, we could have been gone."

"Yeah. Woulda, coulda, shoulda. Story of my life."

The wildlife menagerie picked up in full force now that it appeared the flying, flaming star of the evening had vacated the premises. The gate came into view after many minutes of slip and slide on the mossy path. A steady pulse of green indicated we'd reached our destination.

Where I was hopeful, Rein was pensive. He stood and brooded before the gate, even the wild shrieks coming ever closer, not inspiring him to venture on.

"Um, we should go," I urged, hearing the loud snapping of branches. "It's not like you can call for help, ask Captain Kirk to beam you down another ship or something." Or could he? I wondered as he stared at me speculatively. Maybe I'd just opened my big mouth and sealed my fate?

"No. There's no one to call. I lost my communication device in the forest when you hit me with that bolt. The only other way is on the ship, and that's done for."

What a relief. "So, let's go then."

Even in the dark, I could see his frown. "Don't be so anxious to get in there. You have no idea where we could end up."

"Earth. That's where. We'll figure it out."

A particularly loud growl shook him from his musings. With a great sigh, he bent down and removed a crystal from its perch and moved it off to the side. I knew he'd have to come back and replace the thing eventually.

He took my hand, holding it firmly. "Whatever happens, don't let go."

"Okay."

We both took a deep breath and stepped into the void.

I expected a sliding, swirling spiral, taking us across time and space to parts unknown. I was hardly prepared when my feet immediately touched solid ground, and cool, night air encompassed our bodies.

"That's it? We're here?" I asked.

Rein stared around, one hand tight on mine, the other reaching for his sword. "Stay alert."

"For what?" Everything appeared fine to me.

We were in a forest. The light of a full moon cast a glow upon the tall trees that, in turn, cast sinister shadows. Rein led us away from the gate. I turned back and saw a smooth rock face set into a low, rocky hill, much like the one we'd just come from. There were no pulsing, green gatekeepers around the triangular-shaped opening on this one—not that I could see.

The effects of Earth's gravity weighted down my every

step, making it feel like someone had attached a ball and chain to my ankles. My legs were gangly and awkward, as though not remembering how to function.

"Slow down, holy cow," I snapped.

"Keep your voice down," he hissed.

What was his problem? We were on Earth, not some wild planet with monstrous beasts and fire-breathing dragons. In the shelter of the close-packed trees, Rein slowed his gait.

"Hey, if this is the portal the Kedago used, we should be near my house."

"Not necessarily," came the voice of doom and gloom.

"It wouldn't hurt to look, right? We could at least sleep inside." As long as the crowd of witch burners had left. "We'll have to approach cautiously, just in case."

"That mob is the least of our worries right now."

A small lake with a flat rock protrusion came into view. "Hey! I know this place. We're near my house."

We paused while Rein pondered the area. "You know, I think you're right."

I tugged his hand. "So, let's check out my place then. Damn, this is good. I can get my stuff and my car."

As we got closer to my little house, we stopped and studied it for signs of life before venturing on.

"I don't see anyone. I don't sense anyone either," I told him.

"Okay."

I was glad he seemed to trust my instincts. He did continue to hold my hand and keep our pace cautious as we left the safety of the forest. The house was completely dark. We went around peeking in a few windows before we went to the front door. My hand gripped the handle, and I sent up a silent prayer the landlord hadn't arranged for someone to change the locks. The handle turned, and I breathed a sigh of relief.

"Good thing they didn't lock it on me," I said, meaning the uninvited guests. "I didn't bring my keys."

When I pushed the door open slowly, Rein wrestled me out of the way. He shone his little orb light around and moved inside. "Anybody here?" he called out.

No answer.

I followed him in and shut the door behind us. "Think it's safe to turn on the lights?"

"I don't think we should risk it."

He moved methodically around the single floor, checking each room. There was no basement, so it didn't take him long to search. He locked the front and back doors while I stood in the middle of the tiny living room.

"It's late. I think we should get some rest, and in the morning, you can gather your stuff and pack up your car."

"And get the hell out of Dodge," I said.

The quizzical look I got reminded me he was only a part-time resident of Earth. "Yeah. Probably for the best," he said.

He wandered into the bedroom, and I trailed behind him and stopped at the doorway. I hoped he wasn't planning on taking the bed. The couch was lumpy, and a couple of springs were on the verge of poking through. I was sure he'd be very comfortable on it.

"This really sucks. I liked being here. Too bad there wasn't a way to make things right so I could stay." I meant it too. If I hadn't lost my cool, I'd be going back to school on Monday. I'd moved around a lot in the past few years, and this was as close as I'd come to settling in.

Rein shrugged as though unconcerned with my inferior problems. I guess my outing myself as a witch didn't measure as high on the excitement scale as being an intergalactic space monster wrangler.

"In the morning, I'll go back to the lake and search for my communication device. If it's not destroyed, I'll arrange for another ship to come, and then I'll be on my way." He didn't seem very thrilled about the idea.

"How long will that take?"

"I dunno. A few days to a week, depending."

"Depending on what?" I asked.

"On how fast a ship can be made available and how soon it can arrive." His tone bordered on sarcasm. If I didn't know better, I'd think he blamed me for this whole fiasco.

"It's been a long day, and I'm tired. Not to mention

hungry. Do you want something to eat?" I asked.

"Yeah, okay. Got any steak?"

I wandered into the kitchen and began rummaging through the cupboards with his light guiding my way. "How about a sandwich?" I grabbed a bottle of wine and a couple of glasses and put them on the table. "You pour, I'll cook."

He grunted while I pulled out some eggs and a chunk of ham. I toasted the bread and melted some cheese over the sizzling eggs while the ham warmed on the other side of the frying pan. After dishing it out, I set two plates down and took a seat across from him. He raised what I assumed to be an impressed eyebrow at the food and slid a glass of wine over to me.

"Thanks."

He smiled slightly and tucked in. "This is good."

"Don't sound so surprised."

We ate, and I drank about three glasses of wine. Chalk it up to the stress of the last couple of days. For a lightweight, the alcohol went straight to my head.

"I drink usually don't so much," I slurred.

"What?" He'd picked up one of the newspapers I kept in a basket on the floor behind the table. The beam of his light against the paper illuminated his face.

"You look like an angel." For some reason, this seemed funny, and I began to giggle.

He stared at me. "You're snockered."

"I beg your pardon!" I wiped at my nose with my shirt like one of my schoolchildren. "I tol' you I was tired." My feet felt heavy and gangly when I got up. After two steps, I stumbled, and to my mortification, I wound up sitting on Rein's lap.

"Would you like some help?" he asked.

I took a deep breath and swallowed my pride. "Yes, please."

One of his arms went under my legs, and the other around my back. My hands crept over his massive shoulders to link behind his neck while he rose, cradling me like a child. In my bedroom, he laid me down on my bed. I sat up, reaching for my shoes, but he guided me back down and pulled off my shoes himself.

"Good night, Petal," he said, heading for the door.

"Wait." I sat up quickly, suddenly not so anxious to banish him to the couch.

He paused at the door. "Everything will be fine. You don't need to worry." His tone was soothing, and for some reason, I believed him.

"Can…can you sit with me for a while?"

He came back over and sat down on the side of the bed. "Lay down, and I'll stay 'til you fall asleep."

"I'm not a baby."

"I know you're not."

He'd left his light in the kitchen, but I could make out

most of his features in the dimness. The light of the moon through the window glinted off his white teeth when he smiled. The way he looked at me when he spoke those few words told me the attraction I felt was mutual. Our eyes met and held. I gulped.

Would he stay? Make mad, passionate love to me all night? Just the thought of his hands on me made me tingly. I wasn't a virgin. I'd done the deed before. And staring at the man beside me, I was feeling inclined to do it again.

He bent toward me, and our lips met in a sweet, soft kiss. I sighed in his mouth and felt a zing of friction when his tongue brushed against my lower lip.

"Nice," I said. "You're very nice."

"I've never been called that before." He took hold of my hips, his firm grip reminding me how strong he was. I couldn't help but wonder about the size of him—all of him. He kissed me again, then pulled away. "I should go. You've had too much to drink."

"I know exactly what I'm doing. What I would like to be doing," I informed him.

He stared at me through a narrow gaze, assessing. "Are you sure?"

I nodded.

He put his hands on my hips again, and when he bent to kiss me, I pulled away this time. "Do you think we're safe? I mean, what if they come back?" I meant the mob.

His fingers slid beneath my shirt, the heat of his skin brushing against my belly. "I think we'll be all right."

He pulled my shirt up and off, tossing it to the floor. The cool air chilled my flesh, but I was soon warmed by his hands. I laid flat, and he undid my pants. I wiggled as he pulled them down. He tossed them to the floor as well, and then he stood up and started undressing. I propped myself up with an elbow and watched, my gaze drawn from the rippling muscles on his chest to his impossibly long legs.

My head felt a little fuzzy, but my faculties were intact for the most part. I laid back and closed my eyes, being quite aware of what I was about to do. I'd allow the ramifications to confound me tomorrow in the light of day.

The bed sagged with his weight, and my eyes flew open when he began fumbling with my bra. My breasts sprang free while his busy hands worked their way down my body. I lifted my behind obligingly, and my panties went flying next.

He leaned over and kissed me deeply. One of his hands squeezed my breast, and I groaned in his mouth.

"So nice," I repeated. "Oh!" His hot tongue fastened on my nipple, making me jump a little before I relaxed into the sensation. Both nipples received equal treatment as his mouth moved from one to the other. Cool air moved across the wet peaks, making them pebble. I put my hand to his head, watching him pleasure me in the dim light.

He moved his hands to either side of my body, and

I sighed in frustration. I knew what came next, and half of me quivered with excitement while the other half trembled in anxiety. He shifted overtop of me and settled between my open legs. My arms went around him, and I lifted my legs to hook them over his hips.

Slowly, he pushed inside, my walls stretching to accommodate him. He kissed my lips, and his tongue sought entry into my mouth, every part of him invading me. The scent of him, a mingle of sweet sweat and woods, tantalized my senses. Fully inside me now, he stilled. He broke the contact of our lips.

"Okay?" he asked, his voice sounding somewhat smug.

Not trusting my speech to come out in anything but a series of gasps or grunts, I gave a quick nod instead.

He moved then, pulling out slowly, almost withdrawing completely, only to surge forward. Hot kisses covered my neck and the ticklish spot behind my ear before finding my lips once more. His tongue darted in and out of my mouth, mimicking the movement of his hips. I held myself still, not giving in to the desire to thrash my head from side to side. Yet I couldn't let this encounter pass as a mere bystander. I'd wanted this, asked for it.

My toes curled, and I grabbed hold of his rear as though to guide his skillful movements. My back arched to greet his thrusts, drawing him deeper. He took this encouragement to heart and increased his tempo. I had to pull away from his mouth and turned my head to the crook of his neck. My lips parted, allowing me to take deep breaths. I couldn't resist the sheen of sweat on his skin. My tongue darted out to lick.

Faster and faster, he stroked. Both of us locked tight, loath to let go. I felt him tense, and I threw back my head and dug in my heels. Together, we reached our peak. He let loose a deep growl and then gasped. I heard my own cry of release as though from far away.

Slowly, we floated back down. When I opened my eyes, he was staring at my face.

"What?" I felt flushed and slightly embarrassed. I knew I'd been overzealous in my climax. Although I'd never come quite like that before.

He shook his head as though he would deny he, too, felt the Earth move. Instead, he kissed me quickly and rolled to his side, his arms nestling tight around me. Moments later, I heard the deep, even sounds of his breath and the steady beat of his heart. Content, I gave in to exhaustion and fell into a blissful sleep.

# CHAPTER 7

The light of the morning sun woke me. I reached over to touch Rein, only to find the sheets empty and cool. I was alone. Momentary panic overtook me until the rattle of plates from the kitchen assured me he was close by.

How had this dependence upon him come about? Surely not from one night spent in lust?

I got up and dressed in clothes I could find—ones I hadn't taken. Everything I'd packed yesterday had gone up in a ball of flames. *Great.*

In the kitchen, I was surprised to see Rein working a set of frying pans on the stove. It wasn't so much the fact that he could cook. It was more that he'd managed to scrounge enough food to fill two pans. The scent of coffee enticed me to the cupboard to grab a couple of mugs.

"Hey," I greeted him.

He turned to me with a smile. "Hey yourself."

How could he manage to make my legs quiver with so

few words? He was amazingly hot. I'd give him that. And he was a master between the sheets. Definitely, the best I'd ever encountered. Just the thought of what we'd done made me want to forgo breakfast and pull him back into bed. He raised an eyebrow and grinned at my perusal.

"How are you feeling this morning?" he asked.

I poured the coffee and carried the mugs to the table. "Tired and a little sore," I admitted, taking a seat.

His lips pursed into a triumphant smirk.

The time on the clock over the table read seven-thirty. It was still early, so I wasn't too concerned about the lynch mob resuming their hunt for me. Not yet, at least. "Let's eat fast, okay?"

He brought two plates over and set them down. French toast. "I agree. We don't want to push it. We were lucky to get back here at all. The gate must have still been set in the cycle of that full moon."

I dug into my food. "So, if we went back through, we'd be in another place? Not on Kameri?" I asked between mouthfuls.

"Most likely. It's really hard to gauge."

"If the gates are such a problem, why don't the gatekeepers just close them up permanently?"

He shrugged. "They exist for a reason."

"Such as?" To me, they seemed more trouble than they were worth, considering an entire team was dedicated to recovering people and creatures that slipped through intentionally or unintentionally.

"In the past, there were times they were needed to evacuate people from certain catastrophic events. Lives were saved."

I hadn't thought about that. "I guess the risk is worth it then?"

"During those times, yes, it is. Especially when someone important needs to be saved."

"What, like the president or something?"

"Yeah, something like that. You never know when such a need may arise again. Are you ready?"

*Point taken.* We finished eating. I drained my coffee cup and got up to put on my shoes.

We headed out to the lake and split up to search for his communication device. He'd described it as palm-sized, rectangular, and silver. It shouldn't be too hard to find.

After about ten minutes, I began to grow anxious. "Anything?"

"No," he said, frustrated. "I can't get out of here without it."

That might not be such a bad thing. "You can always come with me," I offered.

We could be a couple of outcast renegades making our way in the world together. Spending our days eking out a living doing odd jobs and our nights beneath the stars, keeping our naked bodies warm with lots of wild sex. I let the thought linger in my mind until Rein broke through my daze.

"Found it!"

I was relieved and disappointed simultaneously. He came up beside me and showed me the device. A bit of static emitted from it as he fiddled with a few buttons, and then a voice sounded. He wandered several steps away, trying to clear the reception. Soon, he was speaking, giving information about what had transpired on Kameri and then giving what I assumed were coordinates of his location. He signed off.

"All set?" I asked.

"Yeah. Like I figured, it'll be a couple of days 'til they can get someone here. At least there should be a ship in the vicinity, and I won't have to wait for one to come from my planet. Then it would be longer."

"A couple of days?" I didn't have that long. Ideally, I should have packed my stuff into my car and taken off last night.

"I'll head into town and get a room," he said, reading my mind.

Probably for the best. "I can give you a lift."

We returned to the cabin, and he helped me pack the stuff I wanted to take with me into my car. There wasn't much. I closed the door and climbed behind the wheel. Rein sat in the passenger seat, his attention on his device.

Being still early, most of the stores in town were dark,

and only a few cars slugged along the narrow streets. I'd miss this place. If there was a way to cast a forgetting spell on everyone who was out to get me, I would have done it in a heartbeat.

"Can you pull up there?" he asked, pointing to the corner variety store. "I want to get a few things to tide me over."

I pulled into the lot and parked. "I better stay here."

He agreed while I scooched low in the seat and tugged the hood of my jacket over my head.

When he returned, I headed for the only motel in town. I parked by the office and waited while he went inside. He came out after a few minutes and motioned for me to put my window down.

"I'm all set. Thanks for waiting."

"Do you have enough money?" Did he even have money?

"Yes, I'm fine," he assured me. He leaned in the window and kissed me, his lips lingering on mine.

He stood up, leaving me with a pit in my stomach. I was gonna miss him.

"Better get going," he said.

He was right. The streets were getting busier, and more people were venturing from their homes. I was glad he didn't ask me if I had any plans. I didn't.

He gave me a wink, then strode across the lot toward

his room. He didn't look back. I swallowed the lump in my throat and drove off. I got about ten miles out of town before I turned on the radio to keep me company. The area around here consisted of small towns and only one local radio station. If you wanted to listen to something else, you had to put up with the static.

The male announcer was chuckling, and I heard a woman giggling in the background. Something clearly had them amused.

"So, what did you say to the caller then?" urged the woman.

The male announcer exhaled loudly and cleared his throat. "I said, 'are you sure'?"

"Did he sound drunk?"

"Maybe. He was talking a mile a minute, so he was probably on something or out of his mind. Who knows? Maybe he did see something." More laughter.

"But not Bigfoot," the woman insisted.

"He said the thing crossed his path just as the sun was coming up this morning. He was way up past the Dougal Mines with his hound, hunting rabbits," the announcer replied.

"And he just met up with this huge beast?"

"Yes. He said it bounded across the path in front of him and his dog, who went bananas and took off in the other direction, totally out of character for a dog who's used to going after five-hundred-pound black bears. Anyway, the dog takes off, and the man runs after it, so he barely gets a look at what he calls *this Bigfoot thing*. He said it had long, black fur, like a bear's, but it ran on its hind legs. And, get this, he said it stood probably over nine feet tall."

"That would make it one heck of a huge bear," the woman said.

I pulled over to the side of the road, my heart pounding like crazy. They were talking about the area up near where I lived...used to live. I knew the caller they were talking about. Old Man Ainsley and his dog, Leo. I'd seen them in the back forty during many a hike. And I was sure as shit they were talking about a Kedago.

Ainsley might be a little off his rocker—the guy was pushing eighty—but he liked to keep to himself. For him to call into a radio station and say that he saw something, it had to have scared the hell out of him. It wasn't totally unexpected that a Kedago escaped to Earth. They'd done it before. Rein and I had made it back to this location. It may have come through right after us.

"Anyway, I expected to get at least one call like this today," the announcer said. "It being Halloween."

"Yes, and all the little ghosts and goblins will be out tonight, so just a reminder, folks, to be extra careful driving."

I stared at the radio, not even hearing the conversation anymore.

Halloween? Hadn't Halloween been two days ago?

After several deep breaths, I turned the car around and headed back to town. If anyone knew what the hell was going on, it'd be Rein. My mind whirled as I drove, frantically searching for the reason.

We'd woken up this morning and gone looking for his communication device—which we found. It wouldn't be lost if it was Halloween because I hadn't deflected his sword-ray-gun bolt until later that night. The night he was hunting. So how could his device be on the ground and not on his person? And my clothes were gone, at least most of them, because I'd packed them up and taken off into the woods to avoid the mob coming for me. With Rein. The next day. The day after Halloween.

So how in the hell could it be Halloween?

Unless an entire year had passed?

Had I lost a whole year going through that damn portal?

I pulled up in front of the office of the motel and turned off the car, not sure if I should risk going in and asking what room Rein was in. I'd seen the general direction he'd headed in, but I also didn't want to start pounding on doors.

Just as I made up my mind to risk it, I saw him. He came out of a room with a little bucket and moved toward the office. Probably fetching some ice.

He spotted my car and came right over to the window,

which I quickly put down. "We need to talk right now," I said.

"Room seven. It's unlocked. I'll be there in a minute." He didn't wait for my reply.

Frustrated, I got out of the car and crossed the lot. I entered his room and began to pace. When he returned, he stared at me with concern.

"Why did you come back? It's not safe for you here," he informed me.

"Well, apparently it is since it's bloody Halloween, and I haven't done anything yet. Unless we've jumped forward an entire year? Either way, I'm wondering how the hell that can be and what aren't you telling me?"

He stared at me for a full minute before he put his ice on the table and slumped down into one of the two chairs. "Shit. There's a calendar hanging up in the office. I saw it, so I know we haven't jumped forward a year. That only means one thing."

"I don't think I like the tone of your voice," I said, taking the seat across from him.

"There's a thing called a Moon Phase."

I nodded. Of course, being a witch, I knew all about the moon's phases.

"Remember how I said the portals should stay bound to the same location during certain times?"

"Like during a full moon."

He nodded. "Technically, the moon is only one

hundred percent full for about a minute. But it appears full for around three days. It's unpredictable but fairly certain that those three days are somewhat frozen during that cycle."

"So, when we came through, we hit the beginning of the cycle, bringing us back to day one of the full moon." I shook my head. "That's messed up."

"I warned you the portals were unpredictable."

"Yes, with locations, you didn't say with time."

"I've rarely experienced it," he said.

I got up and parted the curtains over the large picture window to stare outside. "Do you know what this means?"

He rose to his feet. "Yes. I have to make contact again."

"Why? They're coming, right? You just need to wait. Unless your ship is still here since we haven't technically left to go to Kameri yet. In fact, we haven't actually even met. This is confusing as hell."

"I know."

"So if we're back in time, why were my clothes gone, and your communicator?"

He ran a weary hand across his face. "I guess it's what you'd call a fold-over."

I stared at him blankly.

"Both time frames are meshing right now since we pulled fragments pertaining to us from the future back with us. The place we are now doesn't technically exist for us since we've moved through it. What we're seeing is more or less an echo."

"That doesn't make any sense. There are people out there. They're carrying on as usual."

"That's because they haven't passed through this time yet. This is their time."

"But not ours?"

"No," he said.

I peered out the window again. "So, am I out there? Are you? Is it possible to run into ourselves?"

"I don't believe we can exist in both time frames."

"Then who's teaching my class this morning? If I'm not there, won't people wonder why I haven't shown up? Will I ever show up? Or have I erased my presence from this time just by leaving and coming back?"

"Merged, more likely. Otherwise, we would have seen you at your house last night. Just as I've probably merged with my other self. I'm not completely sure. What I do know is time will eventually catch up with itself, and things should work themselves out. They always do. If we're gone from here, our personas will most likely split apart again. What we need to do is leave," he informed me.

"Leave? Why do we have to leave? Are we in danger?"

Ignoring my question, he began gathering the stuff he'd scattered around and shoving it back into the bag from the store. He'd made himself quite at home in the short amount of time he'd been here.

"I could go back to the woods and see if my spacecraft is there. Although, I highly doubt that it is. If it's Halloween, then I should do what I came here to do—hunt the Kedago."

"Oh, shit! That's what they were talking about on the radio. It was spotted up near my place. An old man reported it, and they thought it was a Halloween prank."

"We both know it's not."

He headed out the door, and I followed him to my car. I got behind the wheel, put the key in the ignition, and paused.

"What are you waiting for?"

I stared at him. "I can start over."

"What?"

"The mess I caused. I have a chance at a do-over, and I want it. I want this life here."

He stared back at me and frowned. "It's not your life, not technically."

"The hell it isn't!"

"You think you're home. That this is your town and your life, but it's not. Not really," he said.

"Everything is the same. I get another chance. Not many people can say that." Right now, the possibility of restarting this day that had gone so terribly wrong was a miracle. A once-in-a-lifetime chance. I wasn't not going to take it.

"Look, we can go back to your place. It's safe now. And you can help me eliminate the Kedago. Then we'll wait for my ride."

"And then what? You expect me to leave with you? Leave when I have another chance to set things right?" He was being ridiculous.

"You can't expect to jump into a timeline where you don't belong and not face the consequences."

"What could be worse than before? My life was over. You saw what was happening!"

"It was still your life. Mistakes and all. We don't get another chance."

"I disagree. My second chance is right here, right now. And I want it," I said.

He stared out the front window of the car and let loose a big sigh. "Fine. I've warned you. If this is what you want to do, I won't stop you."

Not that he could.

His face betrayed no signs of duplicity.

"I'll take you back to my place," I said magnanimously. "You can stay there. I'll even help you with the damn Kedago if you like." I turned on the car and noticed the clock. "Shit. I need to be at school. They're gonna wonder where the hell I am."

"Call in sick," he suggested.

I thought of little Eva in her witch's costume. "Not on your life."

We got back to my house, and I couldn't help but smile. I didn't have to run away! I could stay here. No matter what

Rein said about this not being my time, I didn't care. It was close enough. As far as I could see, I'd gained a couple of days and a second chance.

The first thing I did was call the school. I talked to the secretary, a sweet, older woman named Mrs. Collins. I told her I was having a bit of car trouble and running late this morning, but I'd be in soon. She assured me Mr. Gains, the principal, would be more than happy to take my class until I arrived.

I was practically giddy with excitement and relief as I hung up the phone.

"No problem," I said to Rein. "I can help you out, and then head into class."

He didn't appear thrilled but nodded in agreement.

He grabbed his sword, sliding it into the sheath on his back, and we headed out into the forest.

"I wonder if I should unpack my car this morning or when I get home later? I don't want the other teachers seeing my car in the lot and wondering why it's so full of stuff. On the other hand, I don't know if I want more of a delay getting to work. I still need to put on my Halloween costume. I remember the kids being so excited about today. And little Eva! She's such a sweetheart." I knew I was blathering on, but I was hyped at a second chance. "Think it's a good idea to unpack now or to wait?"

Another nod. He obviously wasn't listening to me.

He was moody about my decision to stay and probably just pissed that I wouldn't be forced into helping him slay more dragons.

We stopped at the lake, and he searched for tracks.

"The last time this happened, I didn't see signs of anything until later in the afternoon. And I didn't have an actual sighting until almost dark," he informed me.

I remembered. I'd been dangling my toes in the water, pondering my fate, when flashes of light interrupted my thoughts. "If you didn't actually find it until tonight, maybe you should wait it out at my place, and I'll go to school. When I get home, we'll go together if you like."

I didn't want to stay here all day on the off-chance he might find it a little sooner. We both knew how things played out. They could play out the same way again, minus the mob out for my blood tomorrow.

"I was hoping to end this now, but if you'd rather wait..." he said.

"I don't see that it'll make any difference."

He laughed without mirth. "We have no idea how things will go now. Not really. Not since we've shown up out of the blue and messed things up."

"But we don't know that for sure. Maybe things will be better this time around because we know what to expect," I argued.

He shrugged. "Just prepare yourself. Not everything

may go the way you want."

I couldn't mistake the warning in his tone. "Just make sure you don't pull something that'll make things go your way," I said, narrowing my eyes at him. I wouldn't put it past him to deliberately mess things up for me, thereby forcing me to go with him.

He stared at me innocently. "Wouldn't dream of it."

"So, what do you want to do?"

"Why don't you head back? I don't really need any help," he said.

I snorted.

"What's that supposed to mean?"

I'd bruised his ego again. "Nothing," I assured him.

"You know, I've been doing this job for years. On my own."

"That's why you had to kidnap me to help you, then?" It slipped out of my mouth before I could stop it.

He stared at me for a moment, his mouth opening and closing like he was going to speak, but he changed his mind. "I won't deny that you helped with the Kedago. And the dragon," he admitted. "But if you hadn't butted in both times, I could have handled it."

The audacity of him. Now it was my turn to be momentarily speechless. "If that's what you need to believe, so be it," I finally retaliated.

The sound of something shuffling around in the brush

made us both jerk in that direction. Rein raised his hand for silence and slowly reached over his shoulder to latch onto his sword. Remembering how I'd subdued the beast the last time, I bent and dug my fingers into the soil. Before I could obtain a feather, something burst from the trees. It wasn't the Kedago, but Old Man Ainsley.

"Run!" he hollered as he barreled past us, his dog flouncing at his side.

"I don't have time to do a spell," I yelled to Rein.

"Then run," he yelled back. He took up a battle-ready stance, legs spread wide, both hands on his sword aimed at the woods.

I didn't run but backed up, giving him enough space to do battle. In the meantime, I held fast to my clump of dirt and began waving around for a feather. I entertained the idea of deflecting the charging beast with a push-back, the way I'd deflected Rein's laser bolt and the dragon's fire. But the Kedago wouldn't be spewing lasers or fire. At least, I didn't think so. Rein had warned me things might be different here.

Loud crashing sounds came from the forest, as though the beast had axes for arms and was clearing a path of destruction. I recalled the beast had been quite large and sported long talons for fingers.

"I thought you weren't supposed to see it until tonight," I called out to Rein.

"Like I said...." He didn't have time to finish his

sentence. The Kedago burst from the woods and headed straight for him. I had to admire Rein's strength in that moment. Several hundred pounds of fur and claws and snarl were coming at him full tilt, and he didn't even flinch.

Where the hell was my feather?

# CHAPTER 8

As before, Rein fired laser bolts, which did nothing but singe the fur of the charging beast. The distance between them was much shorter this time, and soon he abandoned the bolts and resorted to old-fashioned sword fighting. The Kedago, with an arsenal of built-in weapons, parlayed each blow and handed out many of its own. Rein handled himself admirably, but I could see he was well-matched, and I could only guess the stamina the beast possessed. Soon one would tire, and the fight would be over.

I stared up at the clear, blue sky and could see birds in flight here and there. Yet none seemed to be willing to give up a feather to me. I had to think of something else. Last time, Rein had beheaded the beast without hesitation, so I knew I could use deadly force. Unfortunately, with the proximity of the pair, I dared not risk it.

I raised both my hands to the sky. "Ventus, ventus."

The wind was supposed to kick up with this spell, and

turning my arms just so, I'd be able to direct a mini-tornado at the duo and knock them to the ground. From there, I'd make it up as I went along.

But nothing happened.

I chanted louder and really put the swing into my arms, concentrating with all my might. I should have been able to conjure up something fierce by now. It was an easy spell, one of the first I'd learned. Came in handy when trapped in an alleyway with nasty boys spewing insults and slinging stones — a usual occurrence during my childhood.

Frustrated, I dropped my arms and searched the ground for something to use as a weapon. There weren't any sticks thick enough to use efficiently as a club, so I settled on snagging a palm-sized rock for each hand. Easing closer to the battle, I pitched my weapons one after the other, nailing the beast square in the forehead both times. My magic might be off, but my aim was still good. The monster shook his head, momentarily stunned, giving Rein just the advantage he needed to drive home his weapon.

A great roar went up. The Kedago stumbled to one knee but reached out as it fell and, with a mighty paw, sliced its claws across Rein's chest. Streaks of red appeared, but Rein seemed not to notice as he raised his sword high and cut off the beast's head.

He sheathed his weapon and put a hand to his chest as the thing disintegrated.

I hurried over to him. "Are you okay?" A stupid question, I knew, seeing the fabric of his shirt becoming soaked in blood.

"Yeah. Help me get back to the house, and I'll deal with it there." He spoke through gritted teeth, and I felt him shudder as I slipped his arm over my shoulder and began leading him home.

Once inside, I got him seated at the kitchen table. "Take off your shirt if you can," I told him as I ran the hot water and stuck a clean tea towel under the flow.

I filled a bowl with water and set it on the table, holding the wet cloth in my hand. The blood flow had slowed and begun to congeal, a good sign, but the gashes appeared deep.

"You may need stitches," I said, dabbing gently at the wounds, trying to get a better look.

"Can you sew?" he asked. His face was pale.

"You're kidding, right? You need to go to the hospital. You need antibiotics and maybe a rabies shot."

He shook his head. "No. No hospitals."

"I can't fix this here. I mean, I can cook up some herbal remedy stuff, but you need something stronger."

"No. Think about it. I have no identification, no insurance. They'd ask a lot of questions I'm not prepared to answer."

He had a point.

"Can't you work your magic? Do some spell, seal the

wounds, or something?"

"I don't know. I tried doing magic out there to help you—the spell I used before to calm the wild beast. But it didn't work. And I tried another, an easier spell to whip up the wind, and that one failed too. I think my powers are off."

He nodded. "It's possible. Just one of the many things that could be different here." Sweat beaded his forehead. Though he sounded calm and rational, I knew he was struggling.

"Tell me what to do."

"Have you got anything stronger than wine?"

"In my world, I keep a bottle of whisky in a cabinet in the living room."

"Get it," he said.

I went to retrieve the bottle and returned a moment later. "Lucky you." I set the whiskey on the table.

"Boil some water and find a needle and thread," he instructed. He opened the whiskey and took a long swig. "I'm going to lay on the couch. You need me to be flat when you're stitching."

He went into the living room with the bottle tight in his fist. I turned on the kettle and searched for a needle and thread. When I joined him, he was lying on the couch.

"Ready?" he asked.

I nodded and held up the needle. "It's sterilized."

I knelt at his side. For a second, I was tempted to take a

swig of whiskey myself. But I needed a steady hand and head for this. He closed his eyes as I gently pushed the gashed skin together and poked the needle into his flesh. He flinched.

"Sorry, so sorry," I kept repeating with every stitch. It had to be the grossest thing I'd ever done in my life.

When I was finished, I eyed my handiwork. I'd had to use black thread, and it stood out vividly against his pale skin. Rein looked at himself as best as he was able. His fingers rooted around for the bottle, and I passed it into his hands.

"Wait," I said, propping him up with a couple of pillows. "Try not to move too much. You'll rip your stitches."

He nodded and proceeded to take several long swigs from the bottle.

The phone rang.

"Shit. That's probably the school. I'll tell them I'm sick or something," I said.

"No. Go in. There's nothing else you can do for me. Just toss a blanket over me, will you? I'm cold."

"I can't leave you like this." I pulled a blanket off the easy chair and placed it on him carefully.

"Yes, you can." To further his point, he set down the bottle on the floor and closed his eyes.

The phone stopped ringing. Let them think I'm on my way.

"Damn it. Okay, but if you need anything, call me." I put the cordless phone beside him. "The school's number is on the phone. Just hit redial."

"Got it," he said. "Don't worry, I'll be fine." He still hadn't opened his eyes.

With a heavy heart, I changed into my Halloween costume and jumped into my car. When I arrived at school, everything appeared the same. I headed straight for the office to check in, apologizing profusely.

"Not to worry," Mrs. Collins said. "Mr. Gains has your class." She was dressed like a monkey. I tried to remember what she'd been wearing in my world, which had definitely not been a monkey suit.

In my room, Mr. Gains, dressed as a wizard, was performing a magic trick for the kids. He'd made quite a mess of my desk.

The children cheered when I walked in.

"Oh, come on!" he said. "It wasn't that bad."

"Thank you for covering for me," I said. "I had car trouble and—"

He waved his wand around dismissively. "It's fine. We've been having a good time."

"Everyone, say thank you to Mr. Gains," I instructed the class.

The children obliged, and he packed up his stuff and left the room.

"Okay," I addressed the class. "Our party is this afternoon. I know you're all excited. But first, we have some work to do."

They all groaned and pulled out their notebooks. While they copied their spelling words, I looked around at them. Some of their costumes were different, but I remembered most as being the same. Little Eva was still dressed as a witch like me. And sadly, her costume looked as ratty as it had before.

I checked the clock and noted it was half past nine. After lunch, when our party began, was when Blair was supposed to come in and spew her venom. This time, I was determined I would keep hold of my temper and not let loose on her, especially in front of witnesses. Although, I wondered if I needed to worry, considering it appeared I had no powers here.

If everything went according to plan, I could begin anew. Here. In this world. Where everything was the same, and yet, not. Where I was the same. But powerless.

Rein was right. There would be a price to pay.

The only question, was I willing to pay it?

No powers in exchange for normalcy.

At lunch, I decided to go home and check on him. I pulled up in front of the house and went inside, quietly in case he was asleep. He wasn't on the couch. The blanket I'd given him was on the floor beside the bottle of whiskey.

"Rein?" I checked the bathroom, the kitchen, and the bedroom, before sticking my head out the back door, looking around.

Nothing. And his sword was gone.

He wasn't out front, or I would have seen him when I pulled up. I hurried toward the lake, thinking maybe he was waiting for his ride to come. He'd called them from there, and it made sense he'd probably given them that location to rendezvous. Why he would choose to sit out there and wait when they could easily have notified him of their arrival on his communicator was beyond me. Unless he wasn't in his right mind. Driven senseless with pain and fever.

"Rein?" I burst into the clearing and scanned the area, calling out to him several times as I strode around searching.

Where the hell was he? Was it possible his ride had come and summoned him? Already? I was hurt he'd failed to say goodbye unless he'd left a note. I would search more when I got back to the house. Shoulders slumped, I started back. It wasn't like I'd expected to go with him. I'd made my position perfectly clear about wanting to start over. Even if this wasn't my world.

Feeling something sticky, I looked down at my fingers and saw blood. Not a lot, but enough to make me pause. What if I was wrong and Rein hadn't been picked up? What if he was insensible and wandering around out here? I retraced my steps and found the source of my suspicion. Blood on the leaves of some brush heading into the forest.

I entered the woods and began following a trail of heavy footsteps, broken branches, and smudges of blood. From the height of the red smears left on leaves and tree trunks, it was obvious it wasn't from a small animal. I wound up before the gateway. The one we'd used to get here from Kameri. Flecks of blood were on the rock at the entranceway.

So, he'd gone through.

Why would he leave? I couldn't figure it out. He'd made contact with his people. They were coming. So why now? Unless he'd had no choice. Or he was fever-driven. Either way, he'd done it.

My hour for lunch was almost up.

A battle brewed inside of me. Half of me crying out for the new start this world offered me. The other half was terrified at the thought of Rein all alone, injured and confused. If I crossed the threshold of the gate, there would be no turning back. Would it even take me to him? Or drop me someplace else?

Damn it! Why hadn't he just stayed put?

I hesitated for a full minute, weighing my options, then I paced for another two. I took several deep breaths. Backtracked far enough to snatch a leaf and a small stick with drops of Rein's blood. Then I stalked toward the gate and stepped through.

# CHAPTER 9

One quick look around assured me I wasn't on Kameri. I stood atop a rocky hill overlooking a high-tech city off in the distance, complete with mini-spaceships. Taking a few measured steps, I gauged the gravitational pull at slightly less than Earth's.

I searched the area for signs of Rein's footprints or drops of blood. Finally, I found something. I bent for closer inspection and saw the pattern of a boot print matching those I'd been following on Earth. He was here.

From heel marks and splotches of blood along the decline, I knew Rein had made his way down. I descended the hill, sliding mostly on my hands and feet, sending small stones scuttling in my wake. At the bottom, I followed his trail, taking me to a stream. The bank to the other side was at least ten feet across. Rein had obviously stopped here. Since I detected no other tracks on this side, his trail had to continue across the water.

It figured I'd have to get wet. I still wore my witch's costume, complete with a pointy hat, tall black boots, a black dress, and a long, black, hooded cloak. Regardless of the height of my boots, once I waded in, it didn't take long for the water to seep in through the zipper, soaking my feet.

The water grew deeper near the middle of the stream. The hem of my cloak and long, black dress were soaking despite my efforts to hitch them up. My toes squished as I climbed out onto the bank. This side of the stream was trickier to read. Lots of tiny pebbles covered the ground, hampering signs of footprints. I peered around, trying to pick up Rein's trail. Being water-logged, such as I was, his prints should be heavy and deep and somewhat easy to find despite the stones. But they weren't.

Befuddled, I sat down on a tree stump and pondered. He couldn't simply vanish. He had to be somewhere. If a vehicle had picked him up, it would have left some tracks. There was nothing. Not even drops or smears of blood. Curious.

I'd come prepared for this. I stood and removed the leaf and small stick from my pocket. I knelt and used my right index finger to draw a clockwise circle in the dirt and stones. Using my left index finger, I redrew the circle counterclockwise. I placed the leaf and stick with Rein's blood into the center. I held both hands, palms down, overtop. Closing my eyes, I concentrated. Images flooded my mind. I scanned and searched, relieved when I caught a clear picture of Rein. My powers worked here.

He was safe and alive, though he seemed unsteady and out of sorts...and alone. The images revealed city streets, noise, and confusion. He leaned against a wall in what appeared to be an alley. He'd made it to the city then. But how?

I recalled those little flying ships I'd seen buzzing around the big city. If one of those had picked him up, it may have hovered over the ground and not left any tracks. It was the only option that made any sense.

With the hilly landscape stretched out before me, I could no longer see the city. If I needed to check my bearings, I'd have to move to higher ground. I pocketed the objects with Rein's blood into my cloak. Determined, I started walking again.

The voice of reason reminded me with every mile that passed how it wasn't too late to go back. Rein was in the city, and if he needed help, someone would provide it. It appeared to be a civilized, high-tech society. No doubt they could aid him better than I could. But still, my feet plodded on.

I had to wonder how much my decision to continue was about Rein. In the other world, the cost of losing my powers, even with the chance at a do-over, was high. So maybe it was both? That wasn't entirely cold and selfish, I assured myself. My powers had been a part of me since I'd been a very young child. Rein had only been in my life for days. Granted, the impact he'd made on me was enormous. It wasn't just about the amazing sex.

Several hours later, gauging by the position of the two suns in the sky, I finally reached the outskirts of the city. I'd tossed off my pointed hat many miles back, despite the shade it provided, worried that if I happened to encounter someone, they'd shoot first and ask questions later. There wasn't much hope for the rest of my outfit. I'd kept my cloak, though now it was rolled up in the crook of my arm because my dress didn't have any pockets.

I paused for a moment and swiped at the sweat on the back of my neck. In my world, and in the mirror one, it'd been autumn and cool. It'd been cool on Kameri as well. Here it appeared to be late spring, judging by the blooming buds and warmth. I took a deep breath and went on.

The huge city, though surrounded by nature, didn't look to possess anything of it within. Everything was cement, glass, and metal. Not a blade of grass or a struggling weed dared to invade. Individual homes didn't seem to exist. Rather, mega skyscrapers reached so high the tops hid in the clouds. Thousands of glass windows began to light up as the sky grew darker. Those mini-spaceships I'd seen were everywhere, buzzing around like little bees, appearing to be the main source of transportation. The buildings, however, did seem to have a monorail system linking them together.

People opting to travel by foot strolled the walkways,

their attention fixated on their destinations. When I was spared the odd passing glance, the person would quickly look away. A woman dressed in a snug-fitting, gray jumpsuit eyed my outfit with disdain and went out of her way to go around me. Others wore the same sort of clothing, though the colors varied from black, green, gray, and blue, some of them two-piece.

Rein was nowhere to be seen, and the area I'd glimpsed could have passed for any of the streets and alleyways I saw now. I ducked down a vacant lane and slipped into the alcove of a doorway. There was no soil to cast my circle, so I had to hope the objects coated in Rein's blood would be enough for me to locate him. I unwrapped my cloak and dug into the pocket to fish them out. The dimming light would hide my deed from any prying eyes. Still, a quick glance in both directions assured me I was alone.

I held the stick in one hand, the leaf in the other, and squeezed. Eyes closed, I concentrated. I whispered his name three times and waited for the images to come.

Seconds later, a scene appeared in my mind's eye. A shadowy room, a bed, and a table beside it. Mentally, I moved closer and scanned around. Not a hospital room as I'd first thought. Plain, though, no personal items to identify it as someone's dwelling. A hotel, perhaps?

I moved beside the shape on the bed and peered down. With relief, I saw that it was Rein. He looked better, cleaner. His eyes were closed. Although he appeared asleep, he twitched about with restlessness. I bent over him, amazed at how clearly I could see him. As if I actually stood at his bedside. My powers were much stronger here.

Suddenly, as if sensing my presence, his eyes sprang open. He stared at me directly, and when I reared back in surprise, he reached out his hand to me.

"Petal?" His voice came out in a croak.

I nodded. Seeing the confusion on his face, I moved closer to him. "Where are you?" I didn't believe he could hear me, but he stared at me so intently I was encouraged.

He reached out, and when he would have touched me, his hand passed through my body. I shivered. He stared at his extended hand, then back into my eyes.

"I'm not a dream, Rein. I'm here, in this world. I need to find you. Can you help me find you?"

"I... The Delex. I'm there."

"Stay put. I will come for you."

A sharp, sudden pain in my leg forced our tether to snap. Rein was gone in a blur, so fast it felt like I'd been ripped from a dream. I dropped to my knees with a combination of pain and confusion.

A dark shape bent toward me, and stale breath blew in my face. "What have we got here? A witch?"

Quickly, I concealed the items I held into my pocket.

The man moved back, and I saw he clutched a piece of

pipe in his hand. No doubt the weapon used to hurt me. Two more shapes appeared in my peripheral vision. There were three of them, at least.

A bit ungainly, I got to my feet. The trio stepped back, giving me some space, but also took up a position to surround me. Some ginger steps on my leg assured me it was most likely badly bruised but not broken.

"Is there a problem, gentlemen?" I said, attempting to sound in control.

"Yes, is there a problem?" a loud voice echoed from the end of the alleyway.

All heads swiveled toward the sound. Another man came forward. He was dressed in a snug, blue and black outfit with three gold bars on his sleeves. I took it to be the clothing of the authority in this world, considering the way the men around me swiftly moved back and then ran in the opposite direction.

"Thanks for coming to my rescue," I said, not that I knew exactly what those others had in mind, but something told me it wasn't good.

The man was tall and muscular, though not as large as Rein. I didn't doubt he could have handled those three thugs, even without the large ray gun thingy strapped to his side.

He smiled at me. "I have the feeling you didn't need my help. The last thing we need is witnesses. Things could get out of hand very fast. People have a tendency to panic."

"To panic?" What had he thought was about to happen?

He shrugged, then saw me favoring my leg. "Are you hurt?"

I nodded. "One of those idiots hit me with a pipe. Damned if I know why." I suspected the reason but wasn't about to share my thoughts.

He moved to put an arm around my waist. "Let me help you. I can take you someplace safe." Before I could protest, he began leading me to the end of the alley from where he'd appeared. "I have transportation."

Where had I heard that before? And look how that had turned out.

For some strange reason, I got the feeling Rein hadn't simply wandered aimlessly into the void in delirium. I had a sneaking suspicion this was his world. But how convenient would that be? He'd said the gates were random. That you never quite knew where you'd end up. And if he was home, why was he sweating it out alone in some hotel place and not being taken care of, considering he most likely worked with the authority in the capacity of monster control? If what he'd told me was the truth.

The transportation the man mentioned was one of the little saucer things I'd seen flying around. It was similar to but smaller than, Rein's...before it had been burnt to a crisp. The man unhooked a controller from his utility belt and pushed a button. A doorway opened, and a narrow set of stairs shot down the couple of feet to the ground. He started up the steps, his hand now latched onto my arm in an effort to assist me.

"We'll have you patched up in no time," he assured me, settling me into a seat up front next to an identical one before the control panel.

He sat down beside me and soon had the ship lifting and gliding forward, maneuvering easily through the labyrinth of streets. My companion had one hand on the joystick, and the other rested on the arm of his chair. He appeared at ease, except for the bead of sweat I noticed on his brow.

Bringing up Rein was an option, but one I felt wary of doing. I didn't know this world or this man beside me, and I wasn't sure how best to proceed.

"Where are we going?" I asked.

"Someplace safe," he repeated.

"Yeah, you said that. Why the need to go someplace safe? Is there danger?"

"For you, yes."

"What, from those guys? They're long gone," I said.

"That was only a taste of the ignorance you'll be subjected to here."

Why did I get the feeling that he knew more about me and my situation than a single, stressful meeting warranted? I studied his profile. A handsome, strong, well-built man. But I suppose that went with his crime-fighting job. Not the handsome part; that was just an added bonus. He carried the brooding look, close-cropped blond hair, square jaw, ruggedness, and devil-may-care attitude off without a hitch. But something about those cold, blue eyes made me nervous. The way his hand gripped the joystick with a touch of too much determination. The beads of perspiration and the faint smell of sweat made me cautious. He was nervous about something. Me? Perhaps. Or was it fear I detected?

My thigh burned, making me turn my attention to it. I placed a palm over my tender injury and closed my eyes. My chant was silent. I mouthed the words. When I opened my eyes, the pain had gone, and my companion contemplated me with a tense glance.

"I think you can pull over now," I told him.

"Your injury," he reminded me.

"It's fine." I grilled him with a look. "I no longer require your assistance. Please pull over."

When he would have turned away, I held his stare captive, willing him to do as I asked.

In hindsight, keeping his eyes from the roadway wasn't the smartest move. We crashed.

Thankfully, both of us wore a seatbelt, and the ship must have been equipped with some defense mechanism because after hitting what resembled a lamp post, it righted itself almost immediately. But not so fast that I wasn't able to use the momentum to my advantage.

While my companion worked the controls and gawked

out the windshield, I undid my belt and bolted to the middle of the ship. Before *what's his name* could holler at me to stay put, I'd poked the exit button I saw him use upon entry and darted off board as soon as the door opened.

Luck was on my side, for a slight breeze blew forth a small leaf from the land surrounding the city. Nature had always been my friend and instrumental in my magic. I lifted the palm-sized, smooth, green offering in my left hand and waved it around my head three times, quietly whispering an incantation. When my pursuer exited the craft, I was nowhere to be seen. I waited a few moments until he shook his head, a perplexed expression on his face, then climbed back aboard his ship and flew away.

The spell would only last a few minutes more. The leaf in my hand now lay dry and crinkled. I'd have to find a kind soul brave enough to withstand my strange garb and give me the directions I needed to find Rein.

# CHAPTER 10

It took more than a few attempts to locate someone willing to tell me where to find the Delex. It took several more tries to locate the place, even with the so-called directions. Streets here weren't named like on Earth. I suppose since most people flew around in a personal spacecraft with high-tech navigational equipment, names weren't required. However, getting around on foot when you didn't know your way was unquestionably more difficult.

Strangers, in a terrible hurry, eyeing me with suspicion and disdain, gave me landmarks to follow. "See that tall, glass building there? Go three streets past it, turn left at the short, round building, then head right, twice."

Whatever the hell that meant. Almost all the buildings were tall and glass or short and round. I supposed I should be grateful they at least spoke my language.

It took forever to finally come across a building with an actual name printed above the doorway. The Delex was in a shady area of town. Dark streets, and dark windows giving a forgotten impression. Roadways were potholed and littered with garbage. Buildings were ages older than other areas of the city. The Delex stood only six stories high and didn't contain much in the way of glass except for a few windows. I'd seen the odd car and maintenance truck — more high-tech than those on Earth, but still recognizable — amble down the city streets, but here all was silent. No mini-spacecrafts buzzed about either.

The foyer of the Delex was unoccupied. Judging by the cobwebs and dust on the cluttered surface of the front desk, I figured security wasn't much of a concern or priority. From my cloak, I withdrew the stick and leaf with Rein's blood and ducked around the back of the desk. No way was I taking a chance on being spotted doing witchery again.

His impression came to me almost immediately. He still lay on a bed, and as I journeyed closer, through my mind's eye, I could see his condition was unchanged. One arm was flung out the side of the ratty blanket covering his body, his fingers twitching as though in dreams. Instead of calling out and attempting to rouse him, I headed back toward the doorway. Like a ghost, I passed through the barricade and stood on the opposite side.

"Three-fourteen," I said aloud and shook myself from the trance.

I opted to take the stairway instead of the elevator,

which looked like it'd seen better days. Once I climbed to the third floor, I ventured down the hallway, my gaze scanning the numbers. Moments later, I stood outside Rein's door. The handle turned when I tried it. I entered the room and closed the door behind me, then switched on the light beside the door. The light had an effect on Rein. His arm went up and covered his eyes, and he struggled to roll to his side. I hurried over to kneel by the bed and touched his shoulder.

"Rein? It's me, Petal. I found you," I said calmly. He was not the kind of person you wanted to startle.

He stopped mid-roll and returned to laying on his back. "Petal?"

I took the hand he continued to shield his eyes with and carefully pulled it to my chest. "Yes. It's me," I repeated.

He was burning up. His eyes were closed tight as though fearful of the light, and his skin was as red as a lobster. The front of the sheet had smudges of blood on it, and when I eased it down around his hips, I saw that several of his stitches had torn.

He opened his eyes and stared at me, blinking several times as though trying to focus. "Sorry I left. I got a message. The gate...set. They said...faster than a ship. I...didn't know."

"Didn't know what? That they could control the gates?" I'd figured as much once I concluded this was Rein's world.

He nodded. "I went through...they sent ship...pick me up. They knew...Kameri. They know about you. It's why...

set the gate…last world where…have no powers."

I wouldn't be surprised if they'd sent the dragon as well. "What's it to them about my powers?"

I laid my black cloak over Rein's chest. Upon it, I set the leaf and the stick — the only immediate pieces of nature I still possessed — figuring I'd need some help with this spell.

Eyes closed, I held my hands over his body, palms up. "Sana eum, Sana eum," I chanted, concentrating hard. The heat from Rein's body crept upward into my hands, warming them uncomfortably. I continued chanting until my hands grew cool.

When I looked at him, he appeared better. Once I removed the stick and leaf and pulled off the cloak, I saw that his wounds were healed.

Carefully, he put a hand on his chest. I handed him a cup of water from the nightstand. He sat up and drank, then set the cup down. "I feel okay. Did you do that?"

I nodded. "My powers are strong here, stronger than on Earth, I think."

He swung his giant legs over the side of the bed. I moved back, giving him room to stand.

"This is your world, then?"

He took a few tentative steps, testing out his weight on his legs. He sat back down on the bed and reached for his boots. I handed him his shirt, and he pulled it on. "Yeah, and we need to leave — now."

"If they came for you, why are you here and not in a hospital? Didn't they even try to help you?"

He got up and began grabbing his stuff. His weapon stood in the corner, the communicator on the nightstand. He fastened both on his body in a hurry. "They told me what they'd done, how they'd set the gate to that other world. They hoped you'd settle for it since it was so close to your world. That you'd settle for a 'do-over,' as you said."

"I don't understand why they'd want me there," I said.

He stood huge and strong, like when we'd first met, and the sight of him made my knees weak. I reached up to stroke his cheek, and he pulled me to him and kissed me quick on the lips.

"We have to go."

"Why the urgency?" I asked.

"Because if they get their hands on you here, they'll lock you away."

"Lock me away? Why?"

"They know what you are and what you can do. If they can't control you, they'll contain you."

He grabbed my hand and led me to the door. Within moments we were racing down the stairway and heading out the front door of the building. We slunk like thieves in the night, building to building, alley to alley, making our way through to the outskirts of the city.

"Are you trying to make it back to the gate?" I asked,

breathless with fatigue. For a guy who'd been on the verge of death, he sure moved fast now.

"If I can get you back in place, they'll never be the wiser. You'll be okay until I can figure out what to do next."

I pulled on his hand and made him stop so I could catch my breath. "Too late...I was seen. Some authority guy...in a spaceship. He broke up what was probably gonna be a fight between me and some assholes. One of them hit me with a pipe, but this cop guy showed up just in the nick of...." His hard stare made my words trail off.

"They hit you with a pipe? What the hell? Why? I'll kill the bastards."

*My hero.*

"Keep your shirt on, commando. The cop guy scared them off. I think the guys were freaked out because they caught me spell-casting. They called me a witch."

The way he reached out and squeezed my shoulders made me wince. I wasn't sure if he was relieved or angry. "Then what happened with the authority?"

"He said he could help me. I got on his ship with him, which I knew was a bad idea, but I didn't have much choice. Once he began driving, I healed my leg myself, which was a surprise. I can do that on Earth to an extent, like speed healing, but this was way faster. Anyway, I kind of made him crash. I jumped out of the ship, made myself invisible, and found you."

"You can make yourself invisible?"

I nodded. "Yeah, but I'd never done it before to that degree. It doesn't work that well on Earth. At least it didn't for me. Your planet is superjuiced or something. I feel like I can do anything here. Maybe even fly." I wasn't exaggerating. My body felt like it pulsed with purpose in this place.

"Shit, change of plans then. Even if we go back through, they'll come for you. Or they'll trap you there until they have need of you. They'll be watching too. Closely. I wouldn't have a chance to spring you."

"Which brings me back to my question of why were you hiding out in a hotel instead of being in a hospital?" I asked.

He leaned a shoulder against the alleyway wall and chanced a glance around the corner. "When they told me what they'd done, I knew I needed to go back. I wanted to warn you. I had to ditch the guy they sent to pick me up, but we were already in the city by then. I thought you'd be safe. You were at school. I needed to rest before hiking back to the gate."

I pondered this new development. "I came home for lunch and found you gone. I searched for you and found your blood. It led me to the gate."

"After the warnings I gave you, why did you risk going through?" His face showed a mixture of annoyance and something else...confusion perhaps?

"I couldn't leave you wandering around wherever you went. I just hoped you'd be on the other side when I went through."

"But it was your chance, your do-over."

"In a world where I was powerless?" The wounded look on his face made me regret blurting that out so callously. "It wasn't just about my powers," I amended.

His expression told me not to bother placating him.

"They wanted me trapped on an alternate Earth where I was powerless until such a time they could fetch me…for what purpose?" I asked, changing the subject.

"When Aelec—the guy who picked me up—told me they'd set the gate to get me home, I asked him what the hell he meant. If they can set the gates and observe the other planets and dimensions like he suggested, then why all the secrecy, and why send me and other hunters out in ships instead of through the gates?"

"Hunters are low on the totem pole, I take it?"

He stared at me a moment, processing my comment. "If you mean they didn't bother to let us know, then yeah, that's it. Damned if I know why. It makes our job a joke. Like they've been sending us on fool's errands."

"What about me then? What are their dastardly plans for me?" I knew I was sounding petulant and self-absorbed, but I had to know.

"Your powers. I don't know what they want exactly,

but I know it has something to do with that."

"Well, they're not getting their hands on my powers," I informed him, suddenly feeling super tough like I could take on the whole world right now.

"They're not getting their hands on anything of yours. We're leaving. I'll have to steal a ship. A real one, not one of those damn skateboards they fly around the streets in. Something like my old ship. That'll take us far enough away to be safe."

He crept around the side of the building. After deeming it to be clear, he pulled me along behind him. I guessed we were off to steal a ship, but I had to wonder...if they could spy on worlds and dimensions, would anywhere we went be safe?

# CHAPTER II

We came upon a high-security base on the outskirts of the city, surrounded by an enormously high fence. Rein pulled the sword from his back and pointed it to the ground. He turned around, using his body as a shield from any would-be prying eyes, and did something to the hilt to make the sword glow hot. Once the blade dimmed slightly, he turned back to the fence and used it to cut the links enough to allow us to slip through.

"That's some weapon," I said, eying the deadly blade as he slid it back into its sheath.

"Gets the job done."

Along our stealthy way here, I'd snatched up as many stray leaves and twigs that I could find. I'd donned my cloak to ward off the cool night air, making use of the large pockets for my collections. We ducked behind a high row of skids as a drone darted past us.

"Can you get us over there without being seen?" Rein

asked.

"I can make myself invisible. Hopefully, it'll work for both of us if we're touching." I pulled out a handful of leaves, judging the distance it would take to deliver us safely and how much nature power I'd need. "Here, take my arm."

Rein linked his arm in mine, allowing my hands to be free so I could cast my spell. Moments later, I disappeared.

"Get closer to me," I told him. "I can still see half of you."

Guided by touch, he pulled me tight beside him, and soon I couldn't see him at all. I could feel him, though, practically glued to my side.

"This is gonna be like a three-legged race," I muttered.

With a lot of gripping, bumping, and tripping, we started across the open field. The area around the small fleet of ships was well-lit. I kept my eyes peeled, making sure Rein remained undetectable as we moved toward the closest vessel.

"Can you get on board?" I asked. Without a controller, I wasn't sure what his plan was.

"It's the same ship as mine. I'm hoping the controller for my ship will work," he said.

I could hear the click of some buttons and some agitated swear words.

"It's not working," he informed me.

I fumbled blindly into the pocket of my cloak and

clasped a twig. "A metta, tes," I chanted, holding the stick toward the ship's hatch.

The door clicked and then swished up. A set of stairs came down, landing inches from where I estimated our feet to be.

"What the hell was that?" Rein asked, impressed.

"A sort of 'open sesame.'"

Just as we were about to climb on board, huge lights surrounding the fleet lit up, turning night into day. An alarm sounded simultaneously.

"Damn it," Rein yelled. "Let's go."

He clambered up the steps, pulling me with him. Behind us, I saw a giant warehouse door swing up. A platoon of guys wearing space-army duds and carrying huge guns swarmed toward us.

The stairs swung up, and the door swished shut. Rein became visible as he moved away from me into the cockpit. "Strap yourself in," he directed.

I took a seat next to him and pulled on my belt. Still not visible to him, I saw Rein look to see my belt was secured before he began working the instruments of the ship.

"This is gonna be a fast, hard take-off. Brace yourself," he instructed.

My hands gripped the armrests, and I gritted my teeth as he flipped a couple of switches and pulled back on the joystick. We jerked into the air. Straight up. Probably hundreds of feet, judging by the gorge rising in my belly. Then we shot across the sky like a marble in a slingshot.

One of the control windows on the ship flashed red. "They're right on our tail," he informed me.

"I can't cloak the entire ship." I'd need a bloody forest for that feat.

He dodged right and left, up and down, and turned the ship in corkscrews, trying to out-maneuver our pursuers. Several laser shots whisked by us, and I feared this would soon be over one way or another.

"I don't know what to do. I can't shake 'em."

The further we got from his planet, the more I felt my powers ebb. I could only sit there, helpless, and let Rein work his maneuver magic.

The radio crackled, and a voice came on, statically at first, then clearer. "Rein. This is Commander Volick. Turn your damn ship around and get back to base."

Rein picked up the radio receiver. "No can do, sir."

"You're harboring a witch."

"I'm well aware of that, sir."

"You don't understand the importance of the girl. Bring her back, son." A gentler approach, but no less an order.

Two ships pulled up alongside us, and another two were right on our rear. At that moment, my spell wore off, and I became visible. Rein gave me a look, beaten but not giving up.

"How does he know I'm on board?" I whispered.

Rein shook his head. "The same way he knows I'm driving, I guess."

I eyed the ships on the viewer screen. "Turn us around."

"Are you sure? I can try to make a run for it." A noble but futile offer.

"If they wanted us dead, they would have done it by now."

With a great sigh and more swearing, Rein slowed the ship. "Returning to base, sir," he said into the radio.

Escorted, we turned around and landed.

Before we disembarked, Rein took my hand. "Do what they ask of you, okay? You don't want to mess around with these guys."

"Aren't they supposed to be on the same side as you?"

He shook his head and undid his belt. "I thought so."

I tailed him to the hatch, and we waited while the door opened and the stairs dropped. He went down first, hands in the air. I followed suit.

A tall, older, bald man wearing an official-looking uniform came forward and stood before us. "Put your hands down." I recognized his voice from the radio. His tone was friendly, but the look on his face was all business. "Glad to see you're doing all right, Rein. We were concerned when Aelec returned without you. Said you were in bad shape, possibly not in the right frame of mind."

He was giving him a way out. If Rein wanted to contribute his actions to an affliction, his commander seemed willing to let it slide.

But I knew what Rein would say. Even in the short amount of time I'd known him, he'd shown himself to be noble and brave and utterly stupid. It was up to me to save him from himself.

"I healed his wounds, but I held his mind captive. He did what I told him to do. I used him—"

"What?" Rein interrupted me. "No, sir, she—"

The man held up his hand to halt Rein's words and looked hard at me. I would swear an understanding passed between us. He was fond of Rein, so was I.

"Enough," he said. "There is no need to say anything more. Follow me."

He turned and began walking toward that huge warehouse. We trailed him obediently.

Rein narrowed his gaze at me. "I know what you're trying to do. Don't."

His words were whispered, and so were mine. "There's no reason for both of us to be up shit's creek."

Blank stare. He'd figure out my meaning eventually.

I turned my attention to the man in front of us. That rigid stance portrayed a backbone of steel and no doubt a long military career. Maybe he held all the secrets as to why he sent out a bunch of men on spacecrafts to do deeds that could have easily been taken care of by way of the gates. And if they could spy on other planets, wouldn't they see the threats coming? Most of them, at least. So why send their guys out on redundant recon?

We were led into a mid-sized office just inside the hangar entrance. The commander and two other official-looking men entered with us, and the door was shut tight. One window faced the outside of the building, the view obscured by bars. Another window, which was covered with blinds, faced into the hangar.

My quick glimpse of the hangar was one of small spacecrafts, dozens of crates in all different sizes, and machines to move them around—not forklifts. One guy had been pointing this metal pen thingy which emitted a blue mist that appeared to make a small crate hover over to a bunch of other small crates. Weird.

The commander took a seat behind the desk and gestured for Rein and me to sit in the two available chairs. The other guys took up a stance before the outer window and the door.

"My name is Volick," the man behind the desk said to me. "You're Petal."

I nodded, curious as to how he knew my name.

He looked at Rein. "I'm glad you're all right. We were concerned."

Rein's expression was guarded. He was annoyed. I

could tell by the way his hands were gripping the armrests of the chair.

"As for you, young lady, what are you doing on Telexus?"

"I walked through the gate."

"But why did you walk through the gate? You were home, minus a few days, allowing you to start fresh."

What did he do? Dial back the inner-dimensional days and drop me there, hoping I'd be pleased as a pig in shit and stay? And how did he know about me needing a fresh start?

"Powerless, the way you wanted me, I assume? That wasn't my home."

His gaze narrowed. "Close enough. And a small price to pay for a normal life, wouldn't you agree?"

"For some, maybe. Not for me. My powers are a part of me. I'm not giving them up for a charade of a life."

"It wouldn't be a charade."

I shrugged. "No thanks."

"I have some questions, sir," Rein said, his anger barely controlled. "Why didn't you let the hunters know you could control the gates?"

Volick frowned. "Though it's been in the works for some time, top secret, of course, it's something we just recently figured out, and it's not completely accurate. There's been no deception."

Rein seemed to consider his answer. "And why her?

What do you want with her?" He meant me.

"You know what a threat she and her kind are."

"I'm not a threat," I argued. "And who are you to decide what I am?"

"Careful, girl," he snapped.

"With all due respect, sir, Petal is right. Not all witches are the same. We have no right to dictate her life."

"We have every right. A responsibility. It is our duty to safeguard the worlds. She is as much a danger as that Kedago you took down on Earth."

I had to tamper down the urge to snort.

"There is a lot you don't know," he said to me. "You think you're special? That somehow you were blessed, or cursed, with the abilities you have?"

A shiver ran down my spine. "What are you talking about?"

He let loose a sigh as though he'd just been asked to recite Shakespeare. "Several years ago, Telexus faced the imminent threat of invasion and destruction. We were prepared for that event. We'd been working on a serum. Used in controlled conditions, it allowed so-called regular soldiers temporary extraordinary powers. We named the soldiers Invictus."

"Undefeated," I said.

He nodded. "Faced with the attack, the Invictus were sent out to fight. A great battle was fought and won. It was a victory for Telexus. But something happened. Something went wrong with the affected soldiers. Of the tens of thousands injected, only about ninety percent of them returned to normal."

"And the others?" I asked.

"It was a disaster. Their powers remained, and they became uncontrollable. When you acquire power like that, you feel invincible. The population began to fear them. They had another name for them — witch. The Invictus had to be rounded up and kept in a facility to safeguard the public. They had to live out their lives in captivity."

"That's terrible."

"It was. But the facility was set up far from the city. It was by no means a terrible place. There was a community, almost a regular life for them there. But guarded and surrounded by impenetrable walls. Over the years, they became almost forgotten. The government figured they would live out their lives and eventually die off."

I felt an *until* coming on.

"We didn't encourage them to breed. But faced with close quarters, lax restrictions, and their superior abilities, it inevitably occurred. We soon became aware of the situation, however, and we were intrigued. We allowed it to happen, hoping the offspring wouldn't be affected by their parents' artificially enhanced abilities. The children of the Invictus were at first thought to be normal but soon began to display the traits of their parents. We weren't sure what to do with them. We'd never imagined the powers would be imbedded in their DNA."

I stared at Rein. He seemed engaged by the story, but I had the feeling he already knew most of what Volick was telling me.

"The children were innocent but still too powerful to be among the general population. We couldn't allow them entry into society. But at the same time, we had an obligation. Living their lives in captivity and condemning future generations to the same fate was unacceptable."

"What did you do with them?" I asked, annoyed he spoke of these people like a science experiment gone wrong.

"The children were sent to Earth. There they could be easily monitored, and if the need ever again arose, they could be recalled home if necessary."

"You mean to fight your wars?" A rhetorical question he ignored. "You said the children were sent to Earth. What about their parents?"

He appeared uncomfortable. "They were given a choice. Their children would be taken and set free on Earth — with proper guardianship — or they could remain with their parents in captivity."

"That's some choice," I said. "What about that world I was just in? It was Earth, and yet, it wasn't." Rein had called it an echo, but that explanation was unclear. "You could have sent everyone there where they'd be no threat."

"An interesting phenomenon, that," Volick said. "Being from Earth, I'm sure you've heard theories about alternate dimensions with varying possible outcomes?"

I nodded. "Yeah, quantum physics stuff, or the many-worlds interpretation. Confusing, to say the least."

"I agree. We knew for some time these worlds existed, but getting there was a problem. Now, thanks to our ability to control the gates, we were able to lock down the coordinates of one of those worlds. Whether we could use that world, however, was something we needed to figure out. You were our trial. And it worked."

"You couldn't have known my ship was going to be fried, and we'd go through the gate," Rein insisted.

"No, no, of course not. We did have the gate set in the off-chance that Petal would attempt slipping through. It just happened to turn out the way that it did."

"And what if it hadn't?" I asked.

Volick smiled. "We would have gotten you through eventually. Anyway, once we saw that you were, in fact, powerless there, the option to send the Invictus through became viable."

If they would want to go. I know I didn't like giving up my powers. But then again, I wasn't living in captivity.

"Glad to be of service," I said sarcastically.

Suddenly, it dawned on me why Volick was sharing

all this information. Why he'd said something earlier about me thinking I was special.

"Wait a second! Are you saying that I'm the offspring of an Invictus? Is that why you're telling me all this?" No way. I had parents. Albeit, they were dead now. And what was that he'd said about a guardian? Jazel?

Volick slowly nodded. Then he watched my face as I put it all together. Patiently, he waited for me to come to grips with what he'd implied—no, what he'd said. In five minutes, he had turned my world upside down. Everything I thought I knew, everyone I had loved…it hadn't been real. It had been a damned lie. I had been a 'responsibility' of Telexus.

I stared him in the face for a full minute. I wasn't about to give him the satisfaction of freaking out. "Are my parents here?" Though I fought it, a small bubble of excitement welled up inside me at the thought.

"No," he said, realizing I had accepted all of this and that I had reconciled the fact of who and what I was. "There was an unfortunate accident in one of the wings of the facility about seven years ago. Dozens of Invictus lost their lives. Your parents among them."

Rein reached over and took my hand, giving it a squeeze.

I swallowed hard. "You spoke of sending us with a guardian."

"Yes. Homes with parents were located, but a guardian

was always close by. A guardian who could hone the child's power, teach them to develop it and control it."

"Jazel." Yet another loss.

Learning my parents on Earth were not really mine didn't make me mourn them any less. Why hadn't they ever told me I was adopted, though? My real parents were Invictus from Telexus. Dead as well. This was a lot to process, and I didn't know how to feel.

"Was Jazel from here?"

"No, she was from Earth. She did know of your origins, however," Volick replied. "I can see this is overwhelming for you."

"You think?"

"Petal, I'm sorry. I didn't know any of this," Rein said.

I stared at him and had to wonder. Our meeting had been chance. He'd only been at the edge of the lake to hunt the Kedago. But right now, I felt bare. As though everyone had an agenda and knew what was going on. Everyone except me.

"Witches have been on Earth for hundreds, if not thousands, of years," I informed Volick, wanting to debunk at least one of his boasts. Who's to say my powers didn't come from a long line of mystic ancestors? I wasn't about to take everything he said at face value.

"Where do you think we got the blood to create the serum?"

"What?"

"It's true," Rein said. "I know about this. The history, the battle, it's widely speculated about. The story goes…a long time ago — I'm talking centuries — a team of hunters were sent to Earth to kill an escaped. A dragon."

I stared at him. "Are you yanking my chain?"

"Your what?" Rein and Volick both said.

"Forget it. A dragon, are you kidding me?"

"You've seen with your own eyes they exist. And how dangerous they are," Rein said.

"Maybe to you." I couldn't help but sneer a little.

"Yes, and the way you handled that thing was the same way a woman on Earth handled one hundreds of years ago. She saved the life of a hunter. The rest of the team was killed," Rein said.

"Seriously?"

"Seriously," he replied. "The hunter was injured, but after the witch — the woman — killed the dragon and it disintegrated, just like the Kedago, she nursed the hunter back to health. The pair fell in love. When it came time to return home, the hunter couldn't bear to leave her, and he stole her away."

"Against her will?" I demanded.

"Yes. Do you think she'd go willingly? Into a spaceship in medieval times?" Rein asked.

I shook my head.

"Life on this planet was hard for her. Even then, we

were highly advanced. The woman's power became even stronger here, but she was able to control it to a point. The government, who the hunter worked for, was awed by such power. They were able to take blood samples from the woman and engineer a serum. When used on regular soldiers, they became super-soldiers. It didn't happen overnight. And not just with the one woman from Earth. The government was intrigued with this power, and more witches, men and women, and even children were abducted. Their blood was taken, and then they were returned to Earth," Rein continued.

"Good grief." There were no bounds to their treachery. "They had no right."

"The threat was out there. Not just to Telexus, but to the entire galaxy," Volick informed me. "A little blood taken, no harm done."

There was no reasoning with them. They'd never see the bigger picture. To them, the ends justified the means. "You said we were monitored. How? Hidden cameras? What?"

"We have the ability to tap into Earth's satellites and access surveillance anywhere on the planet, so yes, cameras," Volick said. "It's how we monitor the gates, among other things."

"And how else do you keep tabs on us?" I demanded.

"Trackers," Rein said.

I stood up. "There's a tracker in me?"

Rein reached out for my hand, but I eluded him. "Relax,

it's not a big deal. And don't give me that look. I had no idea you were a descendant of the Invictus. Up until now, I didn't suspect you had a tracker."

I scowled even harder at him. "It's not a big deal to you, maybe. Your every frigging move isn't being watched." We'd deal with what he knew and didn't know later.

"Yes, it is," he said.

"What?"

He pushed up his sleeve and showed me a small, black mole on the inside of his arm.

"You expect me to believe that's a tracker?"

Rein pulled the knife from his boot and held the blade up to the mole. He looked at Volick, who nodded.

"What are you doing?" I practically shrieked.

"Showing you," he said, and proceeded to poke the tip of the knife into his arm.

"Stop! Stop it. I believe you, damn it."

He stopped. "I don't mind. It's kind of deep, but if it proves to you that you're not the only one...."

"But I'm not the only one, am I? You've stuck those things in all of us, haven't you?" I directed the question at Volick.

He nodded. "My soldiers have them for their own protection. The offspring of the Invictus also have them, along with any person on Earth displaying implausible abilities — those which we have identified thus far, that is."

I had a little mole, just like the one Rein had, on the back of my knee, though. Not so easily seen and not so easily removed like his could be. I sat down again. "And through this, you can see what I'm doing?"

"It sends out a signal that we're able to monitor as movement either on a hand-held device or on a larger monitor. We're also able to remotely view what's happening through your own eyes. We see what you see."

Just how much they saw, I could imagine.

"It's how we saw you with the dragon on Kameri."

"That's a total invasion of privacy," I said.

"It's necessary," Volick countered.

I glared at both of them. "So you've kept the Invictus offspring on ice until you need them."

"Not just that. Like I said, we had a responsibility," Volick said defensively.

"You also said you've kept them monitored in case you had to call them home. You expect to just issue the call to arms and have them step in line like good, little soldiers. And then what? Put them back on Earth or into captivity like their parents? Or ship them off to a world where they're powerless? What if they refuse to do your bidding?"

"What was left of our enemy fled once the battle was lost. It's taken a long time, but we knew one day they would return."

"And have they? Returned?" I demanded.

"Yes, they have," Volick affirmed.

"What?" Rein asked. Clearly, this was news to him.

"Just hours ago, we noted something happening. We're keeping an eye on it, but I believe what we feared may come to pass. There is going to be an attack," Volick said.

"Even if what you're saying is the truth, and Telexus is actually my planet, I feel no reason to defend it," I told him defiantly.

Volick stared at Rein, then at me. He frowned. "But this planet isn't the one in danger. We proved to be too great a match for them. This time they're out to destroy your Earth."

# CHAPTER 12

I couldn't believe what Volick was saying. How convenient was it that Earth was suddenly under attack? No doubt this was a ploy to distract me and justify all the terrible things Telexus had done.

"Prove it," I said.

Volick looked over his shoulder at the man behind him, then nodded to the man at the door. "Let's move."

Rein and I stood up. "To Command, sir?" Rein asked.

"Yes," Volick said with a nod.

We filed out the door, Volick in the lead, weaving us through the warehouse and up a flight of stairs, then down several long, winding hallways until my head began to spin. We got onto an elevator, which took us deep below the ground. When the door opened, a brightly lit tunnel stretched out ahead of us. Volick continued, and we followed him, the two guards trailing behind us.

At the end of the hall was a heavy door. Volick leaned

over a device set beside it in the wall that scanned his eye, then the door opened. He led us into a room filled with high-tech equipment manned by several military-like staff who openly stared at us. It felt like we'd invaded the bridge of the *Starship Enterprise*. I could see why they called it *Command*.

Volick walked up to the largest screen and stared at a bunch of flashing red lights. "Any movement?" he asked the man sitting in the chair before the screen.

"No, sir. They're amassing, though not yet advancing," he answered.

From the screen, I could make out a small, round, blue and white ball that looked suspiciously like Earth. Not far off in the distance, I saw what the man was talking about. Several red dots that I took for ships were gathering just the other side of what appeared to be Mars.

"What's that?" I asked the man.

He stared at me a moment, then looked at Volick. When Volick nodded his head, the man answered me. "Ships belonging to Septars. An alien race whose main agenda is invasion and domination of habitable planets."

"They're heading for Earth?"

"Yes. That appears to be their target."

"Why Earth?" I asked.

"They want the water mainly, but also a food source. Not to mention slaves," the man informed me.

"There doesn't look to be that many of them." Tremors

of fear, mingled with outrage, moved through me.

"Each one of those red dots is a battleship which holds approximately fifty or more soldiers, each one of them armed with weapons that can annihilate dozens of people. The ships alone can take out entire city blocks," Rein said.

"Okay." *Great.*

"If they keep to their method of operation when the mother ship arrives, they will move into position to attack. The amount of destruction the mother ship alone can inflict is incredible. They won't leave the battleships at first, preferring to do as much damage as possible in air strikes. Once the population has been brought to its knees, they'll descend. That's when the harvest will begin," Rein said.

"The harvest? For the water and food. And the slaves?" I guessed.

Rein nodded.

"What are they? What are we up against?" I wanted to know. Needed to know if we stood a chance.

Rein answered. "They stand about eight feet tall. Highly intelligent. Massively strong. Not built for speed, but for stamina. Reptilian."

"Gorns and Sleestaks," I remarked without mirth. "This is who your Invictus army defeated before?"

"Yes. It was a long, bloody fight, but we were victorious," Volick replied.

"What about Earth? You kept tabs on the Invictus

offspring in case you needed them to return to fight for Telexus. But will Telexus fight for Earth?" I asked.

"We will. But we'll need help. We defeated the majority of the Septars in air battles. The Invictus weren't even deployed until we needed soldiers on the ground. Unfortunately, there isn't enough time for us to position our ships to be there to defend Earth. It's just too far away. Earth doesn't yet possess the technology to protect itself. At least, not for long. Not against this enemy," Volick said.

"The gates?" I suggested.

"Not big enough for our ships. For our soldiers, yes. And whatever weapons we can fit through," Rein said, his face grim. He turned to Volick. "Were you able to establish a lock on Earth? Petal's Earth? The one in danger?"

"Yes. That, at least, we were able to do. Even as we speak, I've got teams preparing to go through, armed and ready to fight. We'll be sending them to as many locations as possible since we don't know where the Septars will strike first."

"How long have we got to prepare?" Rein asked.

His words gave me hope and made me adore him even more. The way he said *we* as though he was in this one hundred percent.

"Not long. The Septar mother ship is slower to arrive. You've got a few days, maybe less," Volick replied.

"What can we do?" I asked, desperate to help.

"The witches," Volick said. "We know where to find the most powerful ones. They may listen to you. You need to rally them to fight, to use their powers to protect their planet. We're about to send through the Invictus. They know what's happening, and they're willing to fight for Earth. They've faced this enemy before. Plus, this is where we've sent their children. They are also on an errand to convince the other witches to join the fight."

They would be my parents' ages — if my parents were alive today. So, in their late forties. Not exactly prime soldiers, but with their powers, they were still formidable allies.

"I have no doubt that by now, the governments of Earth suspect an invasion is coming. They will do their own preparations. We need to do ours to make sure they succeed. Time is running out. Let's go," Volick said.

My mind was whirling with chaos as Volick led us from Command. We headed back the way we'd come, the two guards still at our heels. Instead of returning to the office in the hangar, Volick led us outside to the tarmac.

"Take a ship and head directly to the closest gate," Volick said to Rein. Volick turned to me, his face grim, though he smiled tightly. "A few days ago, your biggest worry was that you'd revealed yourself to be a witch. It's kind of ironic that Earth will, in part, need to rely on that which they fear in order to assure their survival."

I couldn't imagine Blair ever owing me a debt of

gratitude.

Volick and I stared at each other for a moment. "I guess I should thank you," I said to him. "I don't agree with what your people did in the past, but I understand it."

"In times of warfare, men and women do things they wouldn't consider in times of peace," he said.

"And these are desperate times," I said.

He handed Rein a small, square device that fit into his large palm. "On here, you'll find the locations of the most powerful witches. Hopefully, you two can get them to use their powers to fight for Earth."

"We'll do our best, sir," Rein said.

I didn't quite understand why Earth's survival was so important to Telexus. Maybe because it was where they'd sent the children of the Invictus. Or maybe because we harbored people with special abilities that they might one day need for their own survival—again. Whatever their reasons, right now, I was grateful for the heads-up of the threat we faced and for the help they were offering.

"Use the gates on Earth to travel from location to location. It will be faster," Volick instructed as we climbed aboard Rein's ship. "We'll be aware of your location and where you're heading, so we'll attempt to manually set the gates to your next destinations."

Rein nodded. "Thank you, sir."

"Rein, good luck, son," Volick said.

We got on board and fastened our belts. I looked at Rein. "I don't know about this. What if it's all a load of crap? Can we trust that guy? He says he wants to save Earth and blah, blah, blah. But what if he's really just full of shit? Maybe it's a trick to get me and all the other Invictus into that other dimension where we're powerless and lock us in for good? Or what if he's got some other agenda?"

Rein started up the ship, and we took off. He stared out the windshield. "He's not, and he doesn't," he finally said.

"And how do you know? Like for sure?" I asked.

"'Cause he's my father."

# CHAPTER 13

It wasn't much later when Rein landed the ship, and we disembarked in a clearing near our destination. We'd reached the outer limits of the city a while ago, and now we were in a thick forest, the trees too tightly packed to fly through. After we hiked for about ten minutes, we came upon a slight incline with a huge tree perched overtop. There was a wide-mouthed gap in the slope, guarded on all sides by long, dangling roots mingled with soil and fist-sized rocks.

"The gate, I presume?" We'd have to crawl through this one.

"Yeah. Don't worry, I'll go first," Rein assured me.

"Damn right."

He took out the palm light he'd used in my world and turned it on, then he shut off the glow of his sword, which we'd been using to light our way since we left the ship. With only the small beacon of light now shining, the woods were even darker and the gateway more sinister looking.

"They've set this one for Earth. My Earth?" I asked.

"So they've said."

That didn't sound all that comforting.

"Why is there no one here? Volick said they were sending through soldiers and the Invictus."

"There are several gateways on this planet. Command is set up beside the largest in the area. It'll be easier to send them through there, especially if they can manually set the gate to different locations on Earth. That way, they're not hauling their gear all over."

He removed a small, black stone in a niche by the gate and set it aside, no doubt the lock. As promised, he got down on his hands and knees before the entrance and started crawling through. I was right behind him. Just like with the other gates, we passed through immediately. At least, I assumed we had. Nothing much changed except the air was suddenly cooler. It was still pitch-black, with only Rein's small glow slicing up the darkness. We'd crawled several yards and still had more to go.

"Keep going," Rein said, his voice muffled from the surrounding rock and dirt, not to mention his body filled up practically the entire tunnel and his backside was in my face.

We finally reached an exit. Rein shimmied through and got to his feet. I went next and brushed myself off as soon as I stood up.

"How's it feel?" He pocketed his hand device and

pulled off his sword to give us more light.

"How's what feel? My knees?"

"No. I mean here, the planet. Does it feel like Earth?"

"I dunno. I guess. It doesn't feel like anything except cooler." We were still in a forest, and I had to wonder if we'd actually left Telexus at all.

"We're going to have to assume this is your Earth and trust that they set the gate correctly. First things first. We need to find shelter. Judging by the feel of things, it's going to rain."

A fat, wet drop landed on my nose. "Yeah, like any second now. Will that device you have tell us where we are or should be?" This was going to be difficult. We had a huge task ahead of us to complete and not a lot of time to do it.

"It should. It'll be a holographic image and hard to see in the rain. Let's find shelter first," he said.

The woods surrounded us on all sides. "Well, lead on. I have no clue where to go."

He didn't look very sure of our direction either. Pointing over my shoulder, he said, "Let's go that way."

He started walking, and I sighed and followed him.

"Maybe we'll find a road. There could be a town nearby. We could catch a ride," he said.

"No one is going to give a ride to a guy as big as you, especially when you're carrying a sword," I informed him. "And I'm still dressed like a witch."

"Maybe we'll find a cave? Bigger than the one we

crawled out of."

"Yeah, maybe." I didn't want to hang out in a cave. I wanted a shower, and a bed, and food. And a bottle of wine. A big bottle.

We didn't find a cave. However, we did find a hill with a jut of rock sticking out far enough to cover us. Just barely. The space was approximately six feet tall, five feet wide, and eight feet deep, give or take a few inches. We moved to the rear, Rein having to duck a bit, and sat down against the rough rock.

A pile of sticks was stacked beside a small circle of stones to the right of us. Someone else had sought shelter here. Rein moved to the stones and put a bunch of the sticks into the center. He lifted his sword, dialed the power down low, pointed it at the sticks, and zapped a laser bolt into the mix. Flames immediately erupted.

He sat down beside me again. "That should help a bit."

He turned off the light from his sword and fished the device Volick gave him out of his pocket. After fiddling with it, he set it down a few feet in front of us. From the center of it, a funnel of light beamed up, and soon a 3D picture came into view. It was like a drone's view, flying over a town and then zooming in closer and closer until it moved above a house. There it hovered for a bit. The picture flashed and went dark for a second, then we were seeing inside the house. Seeing through someone's eyes. I realized this was what Volick had told me about the trackers and how it allowed them to see what we were seeing.

"This is our mark?" I asked.

"Our witch," Rein said.

"Okay, so how do we find her?"

Rein made some adjustments on the device and set it back down. Now it showed another overhead picture, this one with a line going from where we were right now, leading right to the witch's house.

"Well, that was easy enough," I said, impressed.

"It needed to be stationary for a moment before it could mark our location. I just set it to lead us to the closest tracker."

"How far away?"

He leaned in a bit to stare at the map. "About an hour's walk."

"Do you want to go now? I mean, time is of the essence, right?" After all, we were part of a task force to save Earth.

He took hold of my hand and squeezed. "I feel like we've been going non-stop since we met."

"Well, except for the one night spent in my bed together, we kind of have," I reminded him.

"And that wasn't exactly restful." He looked at me and winked.

"What are you saying? You want to take a time out from saving the world so you can sleep?"

"No. I just want to catch my breath." He put his arm

around my shoulders and pulled me in close. Then he kissed me. Hard.

"You don't want to rest. You want to get into my pants again."

He raised an eyebrow. "And that's so bad?"

I had to admit, the thought of his heavy, warm body laying over me, the feel of his skin against my hands, his lips on my neck, my thighs... I shook my head.

"It's cold. If you want to do it, we have to keep our clothes on," I informed him. "Well, most of them."

That was all the invitation he needed. His hands went to my breasts. Through the thin fabric of my dress and bra, he pinched my nipples into hard, little buds. His lips crushed mine, and he kissed a burning trail down to the neckline of my gown, which he tugged low, so he could fasten his mouth on my breast. After what felt like an eternity, he lowered me to the ground, and we shimmied into a laying position. His hand crept between my calves, lifting the hem of my dress as his fingers trailed higher to the apex of my thighs. Deftly, he tugged my panties aside.

"Plenty of time...to save the world," he grunted as we both worked the fastening on his pants, allowing him to spring free.

"Rein." I sighed as he moved his hand to my hip and pushed inside of me. With one great thrust, he filled me.

He began to move slowly, his lips once again on my

breast. The heat radiating from his chest warmed my exposed skin against the chilled night air. I ran my hands over his broad back and down his arms, which were now propped on either side of me. If this was to be our last night together, I wanted to memorize every bit of him.

His eyes locked on mine as he strove deeper, willing me to come with him. My back arched, and my toes curled as I felt the familiar thrill of climax shudder through my limbs once more. My cry was captured by his mouth, his own grunt and gasp of pleasure mingling with mine as we reached our peak together.

He stilled, prolonging the moment as if he were reluctant to let it end. I caressed the muscles of his biceps and put my arms around him. He held me tight and rolled onto his side, bringing me with him. Nestled in the warmth of his embrace, I slept.

# CHAPTER 14

We headed out as soon as the sun began to rise. Rein assured me he'd memorized the map and the direction we had to take to find our witch. I stared at his back for a while as we slumped through the wet forest.

"What are we supposed to do? Knock on the front door and say, 'Hey, we know you're a witch. We've been following a tracker placed inside you by the authority of Telexus—a planet far, far away. And we need you to help us save planet Earth'?"

Rein shrugged. "We could knock on the back door instead?"

"Wow, good one. You're hot today."

He looked at me over his shoulder and winked. "I believe I was pretty hot last night too."

I opted to ignore him for the rest of the journey.

Just as Rein predicted, it was about an hour later when we reached a small, one-story home on a large lot.

"Hardly looks like a witch's lair," Rein remarked as we stood on the street out front.

"What were you expecting? A run-down Victorian covered in cobwebs? Or maybe a house made of candy?"

"Let's go knock," he said, ignoring my sarcasm.

I peered around the quiet neighborhood and hesitated when Rein started walking up to the front door. "It's still pretty early. Maybe we should go into town, grab a cup of coffee, some food?"

He stopped and looked at me. "Time is of the essence, remember?"

Yeah, that hadn't stopped him from taking time out to fool around last night.

Before we had a chance to discuss the matter, the door opened, and a man stepped outside. He bent to pick up the newspaper on his front stoop and stared at the headlines. It took him a moment to notice us standing there.

"Can I help you?" he asked.

For a witch, he was a nice-looking guy. That is if he even was our witch. Maybe his wife or girlfriend was? He was tall, almost Rein's height, dark-haired, muscular, and stared at us with beautiful, sharp blue eyes.

"Hi, I'm Rein, and this is Petal," Rein said, introducing us.

"Hi," I chirped.

"Okay," the man replied. "What can I do for you?"

He regarded us with curiosity, and I also detected a hint of suspicion. We both moved closer up the narrow pathway. This wasn't the kind of conversation to have in loud voices.

"We need to discuss an important matter with you," Rein informed him.

The man put up his hand to halt our advance. "That's far enough."

I maneuvered myself in front of Rein, hoping I'd be less intimidating. Not that the man looked spooked, but he appeared to be getting annoyed.

"We need your help. I know you don't know us, and you have no reason to trust us, but please, believe me, this is really important," I said.

"Don't tell me...the fate of the world rests in my hands," the man said cynically.

"How did you know?" I blurted before I could stop the words.

"Twice last week, you people were at my door, spouting doom and gloom. Your church can't save us. Mankind is treading a slippery slope, and we have no one to blame but ourselves," he responded.

"Our church?" Rein asked.

"We're not from the church," I said.

There was no way he was going to believe anything we had to say. I had to show him we were alike. If I was wrong, and he wasn't our witch, then he had to at least know who we sought. The tracker *was* at this location somewhere, after all.

I bent and plucked a bit of grass from the lawn. Laying the strands in my left palm, I faced the man. With the index finger of my right hand, I circled my left palm three times, closing my eyes and whispering an incantation as I did so. When I opened my eyes, the grass had lifted up. The strands danced around in the air for a moment, then drifted slowly back to my open hand and lay to rest.

The man eyed me. "Is that all you got?"

I cast my gaze around the street, which was now beginning to show signs of life. "For public display, it is."

He contemplated us for several seconds before he moved to the doorway. "Come inside."

He opened the door and went in. Rein and I were close behind. After the man shut the door, he faced us.

"I just made a pot of coffee. By the looks of you two, you could probably use some." As he led us into the kitchen, we passed a small, tidy living room on our right and a den on the left. "Sit." He indicated the table with four chairs placed around it.

Rein and I sat down and waited while the man filled up three mugs. He put them on the table along with a container of cream and a spoon.

"Sugar is in the bowl." He pointed to a ceramic container on the table.

He grabbed a box of donuts from the counter and put

that on the table as well.

He sat down and stared at his mug. "So, what's this all about? What do you want from me?" he finally asked.

"Earth is in imminent danger from an invading army of reptiles. We came here seeking a witch," Rein said with no preamble.

The man didn't seem fazed. "Reptiles, is it?" He smirked a little.

"I assure you the threat is real," Rein said.

"Oh, I'm sure it is."

He didn't seem convinced to me. "Do you have powers?" I had to ask.

The man looked at me and snapped his fingers. A flame emerged and danced for a moment in his open palm.

I glanced at Rein. "Yep. He's the one."

"Tell me everything," the man said.

It took quite a while and a lot of questions. When we were finished with our tale, the box of donuts was gone, along with another pot of coffee. Our host, Logan, sat gazing into the depths of his mug again.

"That's everything we know," I said. "The threat is out there, and they could come at any time. Telexus is too far away to bring their ships in time. It's up to us and whoever can pass through the gates. Will you help us?"

Logan looked at me and smiled tightly. "When you put it like that, I suppose I don't really have a choice, now do I?"

We set up Rein's device to look for the gateway that would lead us to our next witch.

Logan watched the hologram, his expression concentrated. "I know where that is," he said. "It's about a half-hour drive from here."

"Couldn't they have set the last gate we came through to our next destination?" I complained to Rein.

"They're still trying to figure them out. It probably takes a while to set them, and once they're locked in, they would take time to reposition."

"I suppose," I said. "Well, let's get going then."

"What am I supposed to do? Go with you?" Logan asked.

I looked at Rein. "I dunno. Are we supposed to gather them up as we go along, or just tell them to be ready?"

"The device contains the coordinates of about a dozen witches. I can't see us jumping through gates with everyone. Especially considering most of them won't want to go with us."

"Yeah," I agreed. "I can't see that happening."

"If the invasion occurs, I think it may be better to have a concentrated effort," Logan said. "All of us together would make a powerful foe."

"True, but if we're all in one place, what if the reptiles figure it out somehow and avoid that spot? Spreading out and being prepared might be better," I argued.

"You're both right," Rein said. "We can't know what the enemy is thinking, but Petal's right when she says we have no idea what they're planning or what their next move is. If we're grouped together, we can't guarantee we'd be in the right place of attack. Even if your combined efforts are strong, they're probably not enough to encompass the entire planet."

"Your planet can set the gates to the location when they see them moving, and we can all go there," Logan suggested. "You mentioned you have a communicator."

"Yeah, we'd have to rely on Telexus because we know how much Earth's government likes to share information," I said ironically.

Logan nodded in agreement. "They'll deny it until it's too late for anyone to do anything about it. Although, the way people are prone to panic, I see the government's point."

"I have to agree, although reluctantly," I said. "It sucks, but there it is. Worldwide chaos is only going to compromise the emergency resources that would be better spent in preparation for the attack."

"So what's the plan?" Logan looked between Rein and me.

"If you could give us a lift to the next gate, that would be appreciated," Rein said. "And if you want to join us, we could use your help convincing the others."

Logan nodded. "Okay. Let me grab some supplies. You two look like you're traveling light."

"We didn't have much chance to prepare," I said. At least he was kind enough to not mention my outfit.

Logan packed a bag, and we headed out. Driving by car, we made good time to the next gate. Soon we were standing shoulder to shoulder before the entranceway.

"This is it?" Logan asked.

I had to admit, for a gateway leading to another dimension, it was quite unremarkable. "Does this mean we have to get wet?" The gate was a small pond surrounded by basketball-sized rocks. It sat smack dab in a clearing in the middle of the woods.

"So much for the supplies I packed," Logan said. "Most of the stuff is in packages, so it should survive, but I make no guarantees."

"I'll go first," Rein offered.

"What about the device? Will it work if it gets wet?" I asked.

Rein shrugged. "I guess we'll find out."

As he had done with the other gate, Rein unlocked it, taking only a moment to figure out what needed to be moved as a switch. I supposed when this was over, he'd have to come back and reset them all. If we won, of course. Otherwise, I guess it wouldn't matter much.

As Rein waded into the water, I noticed Logan staring at the sword strapped to Rein's back. We could only hope it functioned after taking a dip. "It shoots laser bolts," I informed him.

"So do I," he said. I couldn't tell if he was joking or not.

"I'll go next," I said to Logan, seeing Rein take a deep breath and plunge. "If I don't see you on the other side, I'll understand." I was giving him a way out but hoped he wouldn't take it.

"I'll be there," he assured me. He took off his pack, and just before I went under, I saw him tightening the drawstrings.

As I dunked beneath the surface of the water, I discovered I had nowhere to go but back up. I surfaced and saw Rein standing on the side of the pond between a couple of palm trees. Logan was nowhere in sight, so I knew we'd passed through to a new place. I looked around as I waded to shore, taking in the expanse of endless sand.

"A desert?"

"It appears so," he said. His focus was on the device he held in his hands.

Logan surfaced and stood in the pond, hands on his hips, looking around in wonder as water droplets ran down from his head. "An oasis in the desert. How cool is this?"

"Is it working?" I asked Rein, who was now muttering and shaking the instrument, trying to relieve it of excess water.

"I'll have to let it dry out and see if it starts up."

Great. It wasn't like time was of the essence because we were facing imminent doom or anything like that.

Off in the distance, barely visible through the steamy

cloak of sunlight dancing off the sand's surface, were a handful of large tents. Hopefully, the person we sought was there. The heat was already drying my clothes, and it was becoming unbearably hot. Several minutes later, Rein finally declared the machine was functioning.

"Please tell me it's saying to head to the tents," I said.

He eyed it for a few moments before he confirmed that it appeared so.

"Good. Let's go. It's bloody hot out here," I complained.

We gathered whatever needed gathering and headed out. The sun was halfway through its descent when we halted about forty yards from the outer edge of the camp. Five tents were spread out just enough to allow for privacy. They were large and high, bright red with yellow trim. Strangely, no one was around. Not a soul.

"I'm getting a weird feeling," I said.

"Me too," Logan agreed.

"Is this a witchy thing?" By the way Rein's fingers twitched, I knew he was anxious to reach for his weapon. As cool as he tried to play it, his intuition was switched into overdrive. Something was off.

"Let's advance," Logan suggested.

All together, we started forward.

Suddenly, the wind picked up. Within seconds the sand was blowing in my eyes and batting off my skin like tiny shards of glass. We had to lean forward and walk with our heads down. It was virtually impossible to see anything, and I didn't want to speak for fear that my mouth would fill with half the desert. I reached out, feeling for Rein, who'd been to my left, and once I grasped onto him, I got behind his broad body so he could ease my way.

Just when I felt we couldn't take one more step, the wind abruptly stopped. All three of us gasped in relief, sucking in deep breaths of clear air.

"What the hell?" Rein said.

"Now, *that* was a witchy thing," Logan said.

# CHAPTER 15

As I wiped the grit from my eyes and tried to shake the sand from my hair, my gaze focused on a lone person standing before the campsite. From the long, dark hair and flowing red dress with a gold belt, I assumed it was a woman.

"Our mark, I presume," I said.

"That was some welcome." I could tell by Logan's tone he was annoyed, perhaps wanting to flex his own other-worldly muscles.

I put a restraining hand on his shoulder. "We need her, remember."

He nodded once.

"Permission to proceed?" Rein called out.

"Come," the woman replied. At least she spoke English. Though she was allowing us to get closer, the warning she'd given us was clear.

Rein looked at me. "Get behind me, just in case."

I smirked. "This is my dance. Maybe you should get

behind me?"

His frown told me he didn't appreciate the idea.

All in a line again, we headed forward. Soon we stood a few feet from the woman. She eyed the device in Rein's hand.

"We need your help," I spoke first.

The woman gestured to the closest tent. "Come," she repeated and headed off, not bothering to see if we followed.

She led us through a long, hanging canvas flap serving as a doorway. Inside, a small firepit made from a circle of stone sat cold, a little stack of wood within, waiting to be lit. There were four bed spaces made up on the ground from a nest of blankets, one in each corner of the square tent. Some cookware and bowls were set on a low, wooden shelf.

"Sit." The woman motioned to the area around the fire pit, where she sat down upon the sandy floor. Each of us sat.

"You know, there's an oasis about a ten-minute walk the way we came," Logan said. "If you moved your camp, you'd be close to water. I'm not sure if it's drinkable, though."

The woman arched a brow at him and frowned. "That water is cursed. Many who enter do not return."

"We just came out of it," I told her. "And you're right. It leads to other places, but I wouldn't say it was cursed."

"And why is that?" she asked.

"Because it led us to you," Rein answered. "We need your help."

She smirked. "Fearless trio who travels through water

to other worlds needs my help?"

"Yes," I said. "We just witnessed what you can do. You have power, and both of us do too." I gestured to Logan and myself. "I draw upon nature to enhance mine. And Logan here, he makes fire."

Logan did the fire-in-palm trick for her, and I tossed a handful of sand into the air and suspended it with a raised hand for a demonstration.

"I'm Petal. This is Logan, and that's Rein," I said, letting the sand fall.

"I am Mina," she said, her eyes focused on the grains on the floor.

I could tell she was shaken by our little show. It probably wasn't an everyday occurrence to run into others like herself.

"You say you need my help?" Her tone indicated she was wary of what we required of her.

"I wish we could sugar coat this, but we're running out of time," Rein said. "Earth will soon be invaded by Septars — an evil reptilian race. Right now, their ships are amassing in your solar system, and as soon as the mother ship arrives, they will attack."

"How long?" Mina asked. Her beautiful, dark complexion had turned a grayish color as Rein spoke.

"Three days, maybe less," I said.

She narrowed her gaze at Rein. "You are not of this

world." A statement of fact, not a question.

"No. I'm from another galaxy far away. A planet named Telexus. We are aware of the danger to Earth. We faced the Septars in battle long ago. We were victorious thanks to an enhancement serum given to our soldiers derived from the blood of Earth witches."

It sounded sinister the way he described it.

"As we speak, regular soldiers, along with the enhanced — the Invictus — are coming through portals spread all over Earth, preparing to fight the invaders. But it will not be enough. They, and we, have been charged with locating other powerful beings to help aid in this battle. We need all the help we can get. Ships from my planet are on their way, but they won't be here in time for the initial invasion."

Mina got to her feet and clenched her fists. "It sounds too incredible. And yet, I believe you."

"Will you help us?" Logan asked.

After several moments, Mina nodded her head once. "For over a week, I've dreamed of snakes invading our camp. No matter what we did to stop them, they kept coming."

I didn't like the implications of her dream. Yes, it might just be a warning, but what if it was a prophecy?

A staticky voice suddenly sounded from Rein's communicator. He leapt to his feet and whipped it off the niche in his pants. He fiddled with the dial, trying to get the sound clearer. "Rein here, do you read me?"

"Loud and clear," said the voice on the other end. "Rein, son, it's Volick. The Septars are on the move."

"Damn," Rein cursed. "Copy that," he said into the communicator.

"There's no sign of the mother ship yet, so we're not sure what they're up to. It appears they're still headed for Earth. We'll keep you informed of their position. As soon as we see where they're staging the invasion, we will set the gates to that location."

"Yes, sir," Rein said.

The line was silent for a moment. Then, "Son, be careful."

"I will." Rein clipped the radio back onto his pants and eyed each of us. "It would appear we are almost out of time."

"We've only found two," I said. "We need more."

"We'll have to hope the Invictus have located others," Rein said. He pulled out the tracking device and set it on the ground.

"The device shows a holographic image of where to find others like us," Logan told Mina.

All eyes were on the device, waiting for it to lead us to our next mark. I grew impatient when it failed to work. "What's happening?"

Rein picked up the device, gave it a good shake, and set it back down. "Full of sand," he said, avoiding looking at Mina. Still, it failed to work.

"Now, what should we do?" I tried to keep the whine from my voice.

I'd always disliked snakes and lizards, and the thought of an invading army of eight-foot-tall forked tongues made me want to return to the other dimension where I had no power. But only for a moment.

I straightened my spine and reminded myself I was a fighter. I recalled Jazel's spell with the three hairs and wished the invaders we faced were Kedagos and not scaly-skinned monsters.

"What should we do? Go through the water gate and hope it takes us back?" I asked. Though the air was beginning to cool as the sun went down, I didn't want to be trapped in the desert on the other side of the world.

"No, let's wait," Rein said. "We have no idea where it'll take us. It may not lead back the way we came."

Waiting was hard. Mina and her tribe set to preparing dinner and invited us to stay with them. We sat around a large firepit set in the middle of camp while the others prepared a meal. Curiously, I didn't see one single man among the two dozen or so people. I noted a few young boys, though, along with some female children. The camp had a festive atmosphere all around us, despite our woe-begotten trio. Even Mina seemed more relaxed, perhaps since she had left us to join the others, temporarily setting her concerns aside.

Logan said the smoke of the fire was giving him a

headache. He went off into the tent we'd been offered bed space in for the night, saying he wished to lie down for a while.

Rein was quiet, staring into the flames, and I wondered if he was concerned as I was with the battle to come.

"Are you okay?" I finally asked him, preferring conversation to silence.

He contemplated me for a moment, then leaned back and dug into his pocket, withdrawing a small vial in the palm of his hand.

"What's that?" I asked, leaning closer to get a look.

He stood up, spun around, and lifted a hand to his mouth before he turned back to face me. "Don't freak out, but when you weren't looking, Volick slipped me something."

I stared at the empty vial, feeling a tingle of fear in my belly. The serum. "Is that what I think it is? Tell me he didn't."

"He did."

"What the hell! And you just took it? Without any thought?"

How could Volick do this to his own son? He knew damn well what could happen. Having power like mine was a blessing and a curse, but I'd been born to it and wouldn't have it any other way. Plus, I wouldn't have to face living like an outcast in my world, unlike Rein, if the effects failed to wear off. Granted, I was an outcast in my town, but I could leave and start fresh someplace else.

"This will increase our odds." Rein sat back down beside me. "You said yourself we've only found two witches." Who was he trying to convince? Me or himself?

"I don't care about the odds. If the powers fail to disappear, you will be locked away forever."

He smiled. "I didn't know you cared so much." His tone was slightly mocking, but I could see he liked the notion.

"It's not just ostracizing you'll face. It's living with the power every day of your life. Trust me, it can be a challenge."

"You seem to deal with it okay. You left that world where you were given a second chance, gave it up the instant you figured out you had no power."

"It wasn't just about that, and you know it."

He looked away from me. "Tell yourself you did it because of me, but deep down, you know the truth."

How could I argue? I had struggled with the decision, but not just because of the loss of my power. The thought of Rein, bleeding, confused, and alone had done me in. Even after the short amount of time we'd spent together, he'd wormed his way into my heart and taken up residence. How was I to convince him of that? Convince him that he meant as much to me as my powers did? Surprising as this revelation was, I knew it to be true. But now that he had the chance to be the hero, the savior he so needed to be, I couldn't be such a hypocrite and say that powers weren't important. He'd seen mine in action, and he no doubt wanted a taste.

He suddenly reached for my hand, and I stared into his eyes. The determined look I saw made my stomach lurch.

"I'm not blaming you for holding tight to your powers," he said. "It's who you are. You're a witch, and though you may exist among the normal population and every day is a struggle, deep down, you know who you are. I admire that. At the same time, you need to know who I am. I'm a soldier. A fighter."

"I know who you are," I said.

"And who would I be if I let the woman I'm falling for fight a battle I wasn't prepared to fight myself?"

I smiled at him and felt my cheeks heat up a bit. "You're falling for me?"

"Damn right." He bent and kissed me quick. "You know I have to do this. To be the man I am, to use every weapon at my disposal to ensure the safety of you and this planet you love. Despite the fact, the bastards turned on you the moment—"

I interrupted him with a kiss. "I know. I get it. The old 'a man's gotta do what a man's gotta do'. It doesn't mean I don't worry about the consequences."

"We'll worry about them later. What you fear may not even happen. Besides, we could both be dead within the next two days and your planet enslaved by lizards."

"There is that," I agreed. "So now what? Do you know what will happen to your body? Will it hurt?"

"I'm not sure. From what I remember reading and hearing, there was a bit of...." His words broke off as he suddenly fell to the ground.

"Rein!" I went to my knees beside him and called out, "Logan! Help me!"

Rein's body was tight as a bowstring, his teeth clenched, and his eyes clamped shut. His hands were fisted at his sides. He arched up suddenly as though shocked by defibrillator paddles. Logan rushed from the tent and knelt at Rein's other side.

"What's happening?" He put his hands on Rein's arms, which had begun to thrash about.

"He's changing," I said, my eyes tearing up. All this pain, all this risk, he did it for Earth, for me.

"Changing? Into what?"

"Invictus. He had a vial of the serum. He took it."

Rein convulsed, and foam came out of his mouth.

"Holy shit," Logan said, trying to keep hold of him. "How long will it take?"

"I don't know."

Both of us watched, helpless to Rein's suffering. I held his hand and hoped he knew he wasn't alone.

Seeing the commotion, Mina and some others came over. They stood in a circle around us, whispering amongst themselves. Mina knelt beside Logan and reached for Rein's other hand. "He is changing?"

I don't know how she knew, but I nodded. "Becoming like us."

"If it doesn't kill him first," Logan muttered. "Damn fool."

I would have berated him if I hadn't seen the worry on his face. "I don't know how bad this is gonna get or how long it will last," I told Mina. "And afterward, I don't know what to expect either."

She nodded her head. "He's too big to move." She stood up. "Let's give him room and privacy," she said to her people.

"What's wrong with him? Is he dying?" a small girl asked, peeking at Rein from behind her mother's skirt.

The woman looked at Mina, who assured the child, "No, no. He's had too much sun today. He isn't used to the heat, little one. He will be well soon. Now, run along, help your mother with supper. Everyone is hungry." She gave a pointed look to the others, and they quickly dispersed, leaving us alone. Mina nodded at me. "If you need my help, come and get me." She went off to join in the meal preparation.

Sweat poured off Rein, and he shivered like crazy. For the next twenty minutes or so, he convulsed several more times and threw up twice. Finally, he lay still. Logan and I watched him expectantly. Mina came up and set two steaming bowls down on the seats we had vacated by the fire.

"He is asleep?" she asked, staring at Rein, who

appeared to be dozing comfortably, curled on his side.

"I think the worst is over," Logan said.

"Please, eat. You will need your strength."

Two more women approached, their gazes glued to Rein. One held another bowl and a cup, and the other held two cups. They set them down next to the other bowls and backed away.

"Everyone is curious," Mina said.

"Yeah, I can see that." I reached for one of the cups and offered it to Logan. I took another one and sniffed the contents.

"It's water," Logan told me, having drank several swallows already.

Mina left us, and we both sat down and began to eat, our eyes on Rein. After we finished and set the bowls aside, Rein began to stir. Both of us got down beside him, and when he struggled to rise, we helped him sit up.

"Rein, are you okay?" I reached for the water and helped him to drink.

He took several sips before he moved his head side to side. I took the cup from him and set it down.

"How do you feel?" Logan asked him.

Rein ran a hand over his face. "Like shit."

"Well, you've been through a hell of a ride," Logan told him. "What were you thinking, man?"

"I think he was feeling a little left out and wanted a

taste of the magic we have," I said lightly, feeling relief at seeing him well. But then my belly knotted up with worry again. I couldn't help but wonder if Rein would be different now. Would his personality change with his abilities? What would those abilities be? And what would happen when they disappeared? Or if they didn't?

"Do you feel any different?" Logan asked.

"Not yet," Rein said. With our help, he struggled to his feet. We guided him over to one of the seats by the fire.

"Are you hungry?" I indicated the bowl of stew Mina had brought for him.

Rein seemed to consider it. "Yeah, okay."

I passed him the bowl, and slowly, he began to eat. "When you're finished, I think we should all try to get some sleep. You look exhausted."

He stared at me for a moment. "So do you."

"You gave us quite a scare. That was bad, Rein. Really bad," I told him.

"I know. I had no idea it would be like that. Although...." He reached for my hand. "I still would have done it."

Logan cleared his throat. "I'm gonna go lie down. Take it easy, okay?"

"Yeah," Rein said. "Thanks."

"You're welcome," Logan said, and walked off toward the tent.

Less than an hour later, Rein and I were curled up in

our beds on the floor beside Logan, fast asleep.

In the morning, I awoke alone. As I rubbed the sleep from my eyes, I could hear voices outside. I got up and stretched, then slipped out the back of the tent to find a place to relieve myself. As I squatted in the sand, I vowed we would leave this place today.

When I joined the guys out front, they were sitting by the glowing embers of the fire. "Hey," I said, taking a seat.

"So?" Rein said, a twinkle in his eye.

Maybe it was just me, but he looked bigger and broader than usual. "So, what?"

I noticed they each held a steaming mug, which smelled suspiciously like tea. Rein passed me his mug, and I took a long swig. Yep, tea.

"Aren't you interested in what I can do now?" Rein asked.

"Is that what you two are up to? Seeing who has the bigger dick?" It was early, and I'd had a rough night, hence, the sarcasm.

Logan laughed, but Rein frowned.

"I didn't mean it literally," I said.

"We've been trying a few things, seeing what he's capable of," Logan said.

I contemplated them both over the rim of the mug. "So, show me what you got."

Rein's smile was like a kid on Christmas morning. He

slid from his seat to a kneeling position. Using his hands, he dug in the sand until he had a small, well-shaped pit about a foot wide and half a foot deep. He closed his eyes and held his palms over the pit. To my amazement, it suddenly began to fill with water. It flowed in a steady stream from the bottom up until it filled the dug-out area. Rein opened his eyes and grinned.

"Water," Logan said. "This is kind of funny if you think about it."

"What's funny?" I asked, my gaze still glued on the clear puddle Rein had created.

"Us four. You're earth, I'm fire, Mina is wind, and Rein—"

"Is water," I said.

# CHAPTER 16

The four of us—Logan, Mina, Rein, and I—all sat around the small, cold firepit inside the tent we'd spent the night in. Rein was anxious to explore his newfound powers, but after his little well trick, Mina had come over and suggested we move inside, out of the way of prying eyes.

"We need to leave," I said.

"We don't know where we need to go yet," Rein objected.

I wanted to go home and sleep in my own bed before all hell broke loose. That probably wasn't an option for me now, though. Not when the town was still hot for my blood.

"No offense to Mina, but I highly doubt the Septars are going to attack a desert. There's not enough going on here. Not many people, little water, and not much food. I think if they're going to attack anywhere, it'll be either in a highly populated city where they can do the most damage or maybe in a smaller town where they can contain everyone," I said.

"I have to agree," Logan said.

"So where do you suggest we go? I haven't heard anything from Volick. I think in the meantime, we should just stay put and wait for the heads-up," Rein said.

"I'm going crazy sitting around." I stood up and began to pace for emphasis.

"We can't just ask Mina to go off with us and leave her people," Rein argued.

"No. I agree with the others," Mina said.

"What?" Logan and Rein both exclaimed.

"You're willing to leave with us?" I asked her.

Mina nodded once. "I think you're right, and the attack will not happen in the desert. I won't know where to go if you leave with the communicator before the location is given. But I agree that we should go soon and not wait."

"We don't know where we'll end up," Rein warned.

"They must have had a chance to reset the gate by now," Logan said.

"If that's even the gate we're supposed to use," Rein countered. "Without the device, we're going in blind."

"If they haven't altered the gate, it should take us back to Logan's town since it was manually set. If they have altered it, it should lead us to our next mark," I said.

"Who we won't be able to find because the device is not working," Rein reasoned.

"But even so, it will probably be a place where we can

at least have a chance to fix it. You haven't been able to fix it here in the desert since you don't have any tools to take it apart," Logan said.

"So you agree with them? You think we should leave as well?" Rein asked Logan.

He nodded. "I do."

Rein exhaled loudly. "Okay then. This is a team, so majority rules. If you're all in agreement, then so am I."

"Good," I said with relief. I would just about kill for a coffee shop and a flushing toilet about now.

Mina packed a small bag, which she slung over her shoulder, and bid goodbye to her people. Together, the four of us headed to the oasis. Rein went under first again, and as Logan waded into the water, he chuckled.

"It's funny that he gets water, and his name is Rein," he said.

"It's not that kind of rain," I replied, but it was too late. He was gone.

"I can go next," Mina offered.

"Let's go together."

She agreed, and we both walked into the water and ducked beneath the surface.

When my head popped back up, I noticed right away we weren't in Logan's town. First of all, we were in a lake. Second, the land was different, although somewhat familiar. It was night despite having left the desert in the early morning, so we must have moved back to our side of the globe.

I could make out the guys standing on the shore. Mina and I stroked across the dark water and waded out onto land.

"Is it just me, or does this seem familiar?" Rein asked me while I attempted to wring the water out of my long dress. My boots had weighed me down while I swam, and now they squished with every step I took.

"No, it's not just you. I'm home."

"What? Where are we?" Logan asked.

"They must have reset the gate," Rein said.

"Yeah, but why here?" I pondered.

"I had no idea there were two gates in this area," Rein said. His communicator began to sputter. He unhooked it and gave it a shake.

A staticky voice sounded from it. "Rein? Volick here."

"I read you, sir. What's happened? We're back in Petal's town."

"Things have escalated. The last time we spoke, the fleet was on the move. They're spreading out over North America, focusing on small towns, Petal's being one of them. Still no sign of the mother ship. They might be getting into position, awaiting its arrival on Earth instead of in space. I don't understand it, but that's how it appears. However, this may work to our advantage. If you display a show of strength now, it might make them think twice about continuing with the attack."

"Agreed, sir," Rein said.

"They're coming here?" I couldn't believe it. What were the odds?

"Most likely, they've already arrived." Rein's gaze turned upward, searching the starry night sky.

"We've been in contact with the Invictus and our soldiers on Earth and setting the gates to send them to the prime locations. They're getting into position. We can't spare anyone else for your location. The enemy is spread out too much. We need to divide our efforts," Volick said.

"Looks like we're on our own," Logan said grimly.

"Understood," Rein said into the communicator.

"How many of you are there?" Volick asked.

"Four, sir. Including myself."

The line was silent for a moment. "Did you —"

Rein cut him off. "Yes, sir."

"Damn it," Volick cursed.

"I did what I had to do, sir," Rein said.

More silence. "We'll be there as soon as we can. I'm on a battleship now headed your way. Should only be a few days, and the fleet we've launched will arrive. Hang in there as long as you can. Give 'em hell, son."

Rein cleared his throat. "I will, sir."

The line went dead. All of us tilted our gazes upward to search the sky.

"Do you think our government knows they're out

there, waiting to attack?" I asked no one in particular.

"Maybe, maybe not," Logan replied. "It would be nice to think we had some more help coming. So, what's the plan? You got a place around here, Petal? Or do we remain in the woods?"

"Um, I do," I said. "Although, we'll have to scout it out, make sure it's safe. I didn't exactly leave on the best of terms."

We began the hike through the woods toward the cabin, Rein in the lead.

"Do you think they'll launch an attack tonight?" Mina asked.

I could hear the tremor in her voice. She wasn't alone. I sensed we were all on edge.

"I have no idea," I said when no one else bothered to answer her.

"You've faced these guys before?" Logan asked Rein.

"Not me, personally. That fight happened years before I became part of the fleet."

"So they may have some new tricks up their sleeves," Logan mused.

"Who knows?" Rein replied somewhat distractedly.

I quickened my steps to catch up and walk beside him. Logan and Mina hung back, quietly pondering the events to come.

"Are you okay?" I asked Rein.

"Sure," he replied, not bothering to look at me.

"I mean with your new powers. How's your body feeling?"

"It's good. Actually, I feel kind of pumped."

"That's good, I guess."

He was new to having powers, and I worried he was unprepared to handle what was to come. I wished we'd been given the chance to work with him and ease him into it. He needed to get the feel of the new sensations, not be tossed head-first into the ring.

He did look at me then and reached out to take hold of my hand. "Don't worry so much."

"I'm not worried. I'm just hoping there's no one at my house 'cause I'm dying to change this outfit before we run out of time."

He chuckled. "We've got four witches on our side. If anyone's there, they won't be for long."

"Yeah, I suppose you're right."

We came up to the edge of the forest and looked at the small house several yards away. The place was dark, and all appeared quiet.

"Looks clear, but let's proceed with caution," Rein said.

After checking around, we entered through the back door, which was unlocked. Everything appeared unchanged, although I could sense that several people had been in the house recently. This was good; I'd feared we may have inadvertently entered the realm where I had no powers.

Since we'd all just slept for a night, none of us were tired. I made a large pot of coffee, and the others hung out in the kitchen while I went and changed my clothes. There wasn't much to choose from, considering I'd packed most of my stuff. I found an old pair of jeans, a shirt, a jacket, and pair of well-worn boots in my closet. In the kitchen, Rein had attempted to make us something to eat with the sparse leftovers he'd uncovered in the fridge. We all sat down at the table to eat and plan our strategy.

"What kind of weapons do you think we'll be dealing with?" Logan asked.

"Worse than anything you have on Earth. That's if or when they descend. There's probably only one ship up there since Volick said they were spreading out. But they can do a lot more damage from above. It's possible they may wait to come down until the mother ship arrives, or at least more ships."

"We could have some time then," Mina said.

"I wouldn't count on them waiting too long. Patience is not their thing. We've discovered their eyesight is better during the day. Hopefully, they'll wait until morning before they attack. But like I said, they can launch an attack from above at any—"

A huge explosion suddenly sounded outside. We all jumped to our feet and rushed to the front window. It appeared to be raining fireballs.

"They're after the town," I gasped. "My car is still outside. We need to go."

Rein grabbed hold of my arm when I went to make a dash for the keys.

"Petal, think! They're in the sky. We need to work on bringing down the ship while their attention is focused on the town."

"But...." I knew he was right. At the same time, I felt an urgent need to help those on the ground. Like little Eva. That poor, sweet girl was probably terrified right now.

"Why don't we split up?" Logan suggested.

"I don't know. It may take all of us to bring down the ship," Rein replied.

Rein made a quick check of the arsenal he carried on his body. He passed a knife over to Logan and handed Mina a small weapon I figured to be a mini ray gun.

"Just move this switch, depending on the level of force you need," he instructed. "To the right is to stun. The left is to kill."

"I can only throw fire a maximum of twenty to twenty-five feet. That's all I've got," Logan said.

"The night is clear, but I can whip up a storm if you think that'll help," Mina offered.

"Let's wait a bit," Rein told her.

I went to peer out the window again. "I don't see the

ship. I can't even gauge its whereabouts because the fireballs don't become active until they're about a hundred feet from the ground."

"It's designed that way," Rein informed me. "The ship will be virtually invisible to the naked eye. In daylight, we'll only be able to see it when it's on the move since it cloaks to its surroundings like a chameleon."

"Then how are we supposed to bring it down?" Mina asked.

I could see how frustrated she and Logan were. I was feeling the same—helpless and angry. "Since we can't see the ship, we may as well go into town and try to deflect the fire," I suggested.

Rein ran a hand over his face in agitation. "Okay. I'm missing half the gear I usually have since my ship was destroyed, and my bag was fried on Kameri. Otherwise, I'd have goggles that would reveal the enemy—cloaked or not. Let's take the car as close as we can get, then we'll go in on foot."

We piled into my little car, and I drove over the dark roads as fast as I could. Several minutes later, we reached the edge of town. Everywhere I looked was chaos. The entire town was alive, with people rushing through the streets, dodging and ducking as the fireballs fell from the sky, exploding as they hit the ground. Screams of terror greeted us as we got out of the car.

We ran toward the center of town, where the attack appeared to be the worst. People hurried past us, and some of them shouted warnings. "Not that way! Turn around!"

In turn, Logan shouted back, "Head for the woods, hide!"

We pushed through the crowds until they thinned, everyone either fleeing into the surrounding forest, or making off in their vehicles, or hiding in their homes. The streets where we stood were soon deserted.

"Mina, can you cloak the area in fog?" Rein asked.

"You got it." She raised her arms and moved her fingers around like crawling spiders. I shivered as I saw the air begin to grow thick and white. Then she moved her hands as though summoning the fog to lift and spread out so that it covered the town like an umbrella.

"Wow, that's amazing," I praised.

"Perfect. What they can't see, they can't hit," Logan said.

"Maybe this will bring them down since we can't locate the ship," Rein said.

I peered up at the sky, vainly trying to decipher the craft. The thought of those monsters coming down here with their terrible weapons was suddenly worse than the fireballs.

"How many do you think we'll see?" I had to ask, needing to prepare myself.

Rein shrugged. "The smaller ships hold about fifty of

them. How many descend is anyone's guess."

"Great." I was less than enthused.

All was silent for a good ten minutes. The odd fireball carved a trail through the sky to crash below, but the fog had done its job. Thankfully, none of the locals were brave enough to venture back into the heart of town, or at least out in the open—that we could see. Even emergency vehicles weren't blaring their sirens and barreling toward us. The authorities must have wisely surmised that silence and obscurity were vital. I could only imagine what people thought, the ones peeking through their windows at the four of us standing in the middle of the street like a bunch of dolts.

"Do you think they'll land the ship? And if so, will we even see it?" Mina asked Rein, her gaze darting around.

"No. Unless they do something different, they'll come down in little single-seater pods. Like that." He pointed up at the sky.

Sure enough, dozens of small, glowing lights were descending from above. These lights seemed more ominous somehow than the earlier ones, considering they contained something far more dangerous than fire.

Instead of crashing to the ground, these deadly projectiles landed softly, cloaking their occupant's whereabouts. We could only remain on guard, our eyes peeled for signs of the invaders.

"Stay close to me," Rein said to me.

"Don't focus on me," I told him. "It'll only distract you and get you killed."

A loud explosion to our left made us swivel our heads in that direction. Then another sounded off to the right. This new chaos came from the aliens on the ground, as I detected nothing but more pods falling from the sky. Screams began again as terrorized people fled the targeted homes or buildings they hid within.

"What should we do?" Logan yelled over the chaos. We shuffled from side to side, not knowing where to go first, as the screaming and loud blasts came from every direction,

"Damn it," Rein cursed as an explosion went off not twenty feet away. "Listen, we should split up into twos. You guys head that way. Kill any lizards you see using any means possible."

On cue, Logan's hands began to glow. He nodded, then he and Mina took off in a jog to the right.

"I'll light up, and you use the wind to direct the flames. We'll show 'em some fireballs of our own," Logan said. He kept talking to Mina, his voice full of bravado I know he used for her sake. Soon they were far enough away I could no longer hear him and then no longer see the glow of his fiery palms.

Rein and I moved off to the left. We strode down the streets, passing stragglers looking for somewhere else to hide. I reached down, not missing a stride, grabbing stones, leaves, anything of nature I could find, stuffing my pockets full.

"What's the plan? Do you have one?"

"I don't know. I'm making it up as I go along," he admitted.

I reached out and grabbed his hand. "Hey. You're not in this alone, okay? I'm here to help."

"I know," he said, then pulled me to cover behind a building as a lizard came into view.

All was suddenly silent except for the exaggerated sound of our breath and the lizard's steps coming closer.

"Can you make yourself invisible and distract him?" Rein asked as he pulled the sword from his back. "Then I'll blast him."

He still had another small gun strapped to his leg. "Why not give me the gun, and I'll blast him?"

"Can't let you have all the fun," was his reply, but I knew he was afraid I'd betray my location if I had the gun and fired. No doubt that was the reason he'd failed to give me a weapon.

I dug into my pocket and felt around for leaves. It took me but a moment to do the spell. "Be careful," I said to Rein before I disappeared.

"I can still kind of make you out," he informed me.

This spell didn't work quite as well as it did on Rein's planet. Looking down where my hand should be, I could still see a faint outline, as though I was a stick drawing.

"It'll have to do. The darkness will help cover me, and you said their eyesight wasn't great." Before he could object, I tiptoed around the building.

The Septar was about twenty feet from our location. Rein wasn't wrong in his description of them. The thing was huge, not just tall, but broad and powerful like a wrestler. Faint light reflected off its shiny, dark green scales, which covered every visible part of its body. The rest was covered by plates of heavy, black armor. Its head was snake-like, shifting side to side. A forked tongue darted out of its large mouth, lipless and slightly agape. It didn't bother to soften its heavy pace or quiet its rasping breath as though it had no fear of retaliation at all.

I went wide around it and snuck up from behind, then pitched a rock I'd snagged from the road at the back of its head. Judging by the way the rock bounced right off, I knew it hadn't hurt. It just startled the beast enough to have it turn around. The snarl on its green lizard face gave me a start. Its mouth was open in what appeared to be a grin, displaying long, pointy, white choppers.

I shuffled to the left, then to the right, its yellow and black striped eyes following my purposely loud movements. It fondled its weapon but seemed hesitant to fire. Maybe it only contained limited ammo?

A snarl sounded from behind me, and I saw the Septar's icy gaze shift up over my invisible shoulder. One thing I hadn't really thought about — or Rein either, for that matter — was how to avoid getting hit in the crossfire if a battle took place. No one could see me, so I knew I had to take cover... fast. Unfortunately, my path to Rein was blocked, and now I had another lizard closing in, obstructing my only alternative path.

I took a chance and called out, "Rein, there's two of 'em!" before I ducked low.

Rein stepped from behind the building. He scanned the area, no doubt giving me a moment to take cover. Then he fired. The laser bolt hit the closest Septar square in the chest. The blow knocked it back a few feet but appeared to inflict no harm due to the body armor. While it was momentarily dazed, Rein fired at the second Septar, then took cover again. I sprinted around the first lizard and moved behind the building to Rein. He was fiddling with the settings on his sword, probably trying to gain more power.

"Shit, your laser bolts are useless against that thing's armor," I said.

"Yeah."

"Hold onto me, and we'll both be invisible to them."

"You want me to run away?" he asked.

"Live to fight another day."

I didn't give him a chance to argue. I threw myself on him to cloak him from sight just as the Septar rounded the corner. We both froze as its gaze darted around, searching.

It grunted a few times, and then the other Septar came into view. They communicated to each other in a series of grunts and some weird language I couldn't decipher before they turned around and headed out.

Once they were gone, I let go of Rein and moved back so I could see him. "That was close."

"Too close," he agreed.

"Did you understand what they were saying?"

"A bit. They're our greatest enemy, so we receive some training. They said something like 'enough delay' and something about returning to the ship."

"The fog is still heavy. They won't be able to inflict much damage from above."

Rein's expression was puzzled. "They said something else. Though it makes no sense. Something about the gate."

"The gate? Like the one near my place?"

"Yeah. The word they used, I could only substitute it with 'annihilate'."

Rein's radio began to crackle. He pulled it free and held it up to try and clear the signal.

"Rein? Come in." Volick's voice sounded like it was a million miles away, which I hoped wasn't the case.

"Rein here."

"Listen, son. We've...duped. Turning back. Not Earth...diversion. Mother ship...rest of fleet... Telexus... defenseless. All gates now set... Telexus. Come back." The radio static jumbled his voice and then cut out completely.

Rein looked like he would throw up. I reached out and grabbed his hand. "What does he mean? What's happening?"

It took him a moment to speak. "It was a ruse. They're not here to conquer Earth. They're after the gates. We have to go."

He moved from the cover of the building and began to sprint, pulling me along with him.

"Where are we going?"

"The car. Have to get there before them," he said.

"Where? The gate? They're going for the gate?" It suddenly became clear in my mind. "Oh shit. Telexus sent their soldiers here, and most of their fleet is en route. It was all a diversion by the Septars. That's why they focused on the small towns, no doubt the ones with the gates. If they destroy them, the Invictus and other soldiers can't get back. No one can."

# CHAPTER 17

"Their target all along was Telexus. I didn't think the bastards were that clever," Rein spat.

We reached the car, and my invisibility wore off as I grabbed the door handle and jumped in. I drove, barreling through the deserted streets back toward my place. Behind us, the odd blasts of light were visible through the rearview mirror. I guess the Septars felt they had to put on a show. Or maybe they were pissed at being left out of the real battle and decided to take out their aggression on us. Even if the majority of the Septars were right now invading Telexus, we still had a bunch of them here to deal with.

"After they destroy the gates, they'll leave and join the battle on my planet," Rein predicted as if he'd read my mind. Although we both knew it would be no battle. Not while Telexus stood virtually defenseless. It would be an annihilation.

"So, what? They decided to shoot up the town for

kicks?"

"No doubt to draw any retaliation in that direction while they homed in on the real target. They know they have the Invictus and Telexus soldiers here to deal with and whatever Earthlings can throw at them. When they sent down the pods, they probably aimed a few right at the gates. We might already be too late."

When my place came into view, I drove the car right past the house and across the short field in the direction of the forest. We could then go no further and had to run. When we reached the lake, we saw two lizards moving in the direction of the gate in the forest. We could only hope they didn't know about the gate at the bottom of the lake. Although, that one would be hard for them to find. Even I could only guess at the general location.

Rein knelt at the water's edge and cupped his hands. He rose, holding some water, and tossed it in the Septar's direction, using a wave-like motion. A long line of water shot from the lake, following the direction of his spray. The force of the gusher washed the Septars over onto their bellies. We rushed toward them, Rein reaching for his sword and me grabbing a handful of dirt. He blasted away at them, doing little damage thanks to their armor, but it allowed enough time for me to scatter them with the soil.

I put my palms out toward them and yelled, "Inpetus, inpetus, inpetus!"

The soil burst into flames. The Septars leapt to their feet and ran about, pounding at their bodies, trying to extinguish the fire.

"Rein! The gate. Go! I'll hold them off. You go. Save your planet."

Rein stared at the lizards, who were slowly winning the battle against the flames. They screeched and cried, cursing me, no doubt. Then he turned his gaze toward the gate. What was he waiting for?

"Go!" I hollered again.

"I can't leave you," he yelled, raising his voice over the Septar's cries.

I bent to retrieve more soil and tossed it on the lizards while ducking to avoid their massive, swinging arms. "Inpetus!"

The flames broke out again, distracting them, giving Rein the precious time he needed.

"Come with me," Rein called.

I shook my head. "I can't leave the town to these bastards." Couldn't leave little Eva.

"Logan and Mina will deal with them."

"They may already be dead." I couldn't take the chance. I was sorry that Telexus was in trouble, but since it had come down to a choice, I had to pick Earth.

One of the Septars reached for his weapon. I thought he'd aim it at me, but instead, he aimed at the gate. Rein saw his intent and fired at him.

"Go, Rein! Hurry. Before it's too late." We could only hope that by now, all the gates would be set for Telexus. Anyone who received Volick's message could attempt to make it back to aid their planet.

Rein stared into my eyes and continued to fire. The Septar finally lost its grip on the weapon but not before it let loose one long, fiery blast and destroyed the gate.

"No!" I cried. I bent down and put my hands to the earth, drawing power. "Rein, move!" I yelled, keeping my hands on the ground.

Rein jumped out of the way just as the ground began to rumble and shake, then a deep crevice cracked open before me, aimed directly at the lizards. Both of them, still brushing at the flames on their bodies, fell into the crevice and screamed. I closed my eyes, releasing my fury, and opened them to see the crack slowly close.

Rein came up beside me moments later. I stood up, and we grasped hands.

"Holy shit. Remind me never to piss you off," he said.

I looked up at him, searching his gaze. "I'm so sorry about Telexus."

He nodded once. "Volick is on his way back with the fleet. They're closer to my planet than here. They'll get there in time."

We both could only imagine what they'd find.

"They can't have destroyed all the gates. Others will find a way back," I assured him.

"The lake," he reminded me.

"It'll be hard to find the gate, especially in the dark. You go. I can't leave. Not while Earth is in danger."

After a long pause, he said, "Let's get back into town. Find Logan and Mina."

I knew the choice he faced right now was difficult. Probably the hardest one he'd ever made. "Are you sure?"

He nodded. "Let's end those invading bastards. They'll think twice before they mess with Earth again."

Despite all the chaos, I smiled.

We strode past the lake, through the woods, and climbed into my car. "Things will change after this, you know," Rein said. "You won't be an outcast here anymore. You'll be a hero. You can stay, have your life back like you wanted."

He was right. But when I looked at his profile, I knew I'd never leave him. If he wanted to return to Telexus, I'd be there, right by his side.

"I love you, Rein. Where you go, I go," I told him.

He gazed at me and smiled, reached over to grab my hand and ran his thumb across my palm.

"I love you too, Petal."

And so we headed off toward the town to fight for Earth, and then, we would find the gate to get Rein home to

Telexus, and we'd save his planet as well.
       As long as we were together, I knew we would prevail.

# EPILOGUE

*One year later...*

"Can you see them?" I yelled. The ship swooped and swayed side to side and up and down in a desperate attempt to outmaneuver the enemy.

"Yeah. Two. Right on my tail. Damn it!" Rein yelled back.

We sat next to each other, strapped into our seats, but the commands coming over the radio and the powerful blasts of laser fire all around us forced us to raise our voices. This wasn't the first time we'd been attacked, and it wouldn't be the last.

The Septars, just barely thwarted in their invasion of Telexus a year ago, were hot for blood. They'd pick us off one by one if they were able.

"Not today, you slimy green bastards!" Rein vowed. In seconds, he skillfully positioned us between the two enemy ships, then pulled the joystick back hard, sending our ship, nose-first, straight up into the air.

We both yelled, "Oh, yeah, baby!" as the enemy slammed into each other and exploded.

Rein reached for the crackling radio. "Rein here."

"What's happening out there?" Volick demanded.

"Septars, sir. Annihilated." We looked at each other and smiled. "Heading for home now."

I heard a deep sigh over the airwaves. "Report to me as soon as you land. Both of you," Volick said.

"Copy that, sir."

"I don't think I'm ever gonna get used to military life," I said.

Rein grinned at me. "You said you weren't the domestic type, remember? You didn't want to stay home and keep house and raise kids."

Yes, I did remember. We'd had this discussion once we'd eliminated the Septars from Earth and then rushed back to Telexus after locating the water gate. Then fighting another battle, which was long and bloody and brutal. After it was over, a tremulous victory for our side had been won. Logan and Mina had come with us to Telexus, not even hesitating to fight a battle that wasn't theirs to fight. Afterward, when we'd all returned to Earth, we'd gone our separate ways but would always remain the best of friends.

I'd gone home, and Rein had been at my side. That was

when I'd been approached by a group of townsfolk, including the mayor, who'd asked me to stay. I was even offered my old job back. But staring at the tight, uneasy smiles on the faces of people who'd been so quick to condemn me earlier, I knew things would never be the same. People weren't ready to come to grips with other-worldly invaders, never mind people with powerful abilities. My presence would be a constant reminder that we had nearly lost everything.

I'd told them I would think about it, and I did. But in the end, as I lay wrapped in Rein's arms after hours of lovemaking, he'd asked me what I wanted, and I answered him truthfully. "You." Then he kissed my lips and held me tighter. We'd talked until the rays of the sun shone through my window onto our faces. Over coffee, and after a lot of contemplation, I'd made up my mind.

So now, the pair of us are doing Rein's old job. Guardians of the gates. Or, at least, guardians of the remaining gates. Our job is pretty easy, considering not many gates remain.

Rein's powers never left him. He's an Invictus now. But he, like the other enhanced soldiers, were given the option of going to Earth or remaining on Telexus, but not in captivity, or they could do whatever they wanted, go anywhere they wished. They were free. I was surprised by how many chose to stay. People of Telexus are not so quick to condemn anymore. And when I walk down the street or I'm spotted doing something 'witchy,' they're no longer fearful.

Rein and I live in one of the tall skyscrapers in the city when we're not out wrangling intergalactic space monsters who've escaped to Earth or somewhere else they shouldn't be. Or battling the never-ending Septars who haunt the skies. The township on Earth purchased my little house and gave it to me as a gift, where I could return whenever I wished and live in peace. We use it as a vacation home when we need a break from the pressures of our job or from Rein's father, nagging us to get married and give him grandchildren.

It will happen one day, I'm sure. There's no hurry.

We have all the time in the world.

Juliet is an award-winning author of several bestselling novels and short stories. She lives in Ontario with her husband, cat and dog. You can check out Juliet's website to see what she's been up to. http://JulietCardinWebsite.Yolasite.com